Birthkeeper
of
BETHLEHEM

A Midwife's Tale

Bridget Supple

WOMANCRAFT PUBLISHING

The Birthkeeper of Bethlehem copyright © 2021 Bridget Supple
First Edition: Chetwynd Publishing: Bridget Supple Books, 2021
Original cover copyright © 2021 Bridget Supple

Second Edition: Womancraft Publishing, 2022

Published by Womancraft Publishing, 2022
womancraftpublishing.com

ISBN 978-1-910559-82-6

The Birthkeeper of Bethlehem is also available in ebook format:
ISBN 978-1-910559-81-9

Cover design and typesetting by Lucent Word, lucentword.com

Womancraft Publishing is committed to sharing powerful new women's voices, through a collaborative publishing process. We are proud to midwife this work, however the story, the experiences and the words are the author's alone. A percentage of Womancraft Publishing profits are invested back into the environment reforesting the tropics (via TreeSisters) and forward into the community: providing books for girls in developing countries, and affordable libraries for red tents and women's groups around the world.

Praise for
The Birthkeeper of Bethlehem

We know this story. But we've never heard it quite like this.

Bridget Supple conjures the colors and sounds and rhythms of daily life in Bethlehem at the beginning of the Common Era. From the perspective of the midwife, Salome, it's just another birth. Births are always miraculous, only this one is a little more so than usual. There's a new star in the sky. And there are strangers with strange visions. But the mother and baby are the work of the moment and those mysterious things must be puzzled over later.

This book tells a story we all know with great sweetness and a loving heart.

Midwifery is indeed timeless: a traditionally-trained midwife today would be using the same techniques and medical herbs. In fact, you could actually use these birth stories as a very good midwifery textbook!

Gail Hart, midwife of fifty years, dedicated to preserving improving birth outcomes by integrating traditional midwifery methods with appropriate medical care

The Birthkeeper of Bethlehem is the story that has been waiting to be told. Bridget Supple conjures up the suppressed herstory of the midwife who attended Mary. Anyone who has ever shared a birthspace will attest to the veracity of Supple's descriptions, but for me, the power of this book is that it provides an almost unique window into the universal experience of both birthing people and their attendants. The hidden power and wisdom of birth is laid bare, reminding us that this rite of passage does not change and nor does the care we need and deserve. The Birthkeeper of Bethlehem has ancient wisdom that we forget at our peril. She speaks down the ages to me to keep fighting for twenty-first century Marys to have the same skilled, gentle and loving support.

**Maddie McMahon, doula, educator,
mentor, author and activist**

I love this book! It lulled me gently into a world my bones remember; then left me weeping cool tears that washed clear my soul. The reading of the book was a ceremony in itself; a love story to the skilled hands and open hearts that have always welcomed the first breath and witnessed the last breath; for as long as humans have lived in community there have been the midwives.
Thank you, Bridget, for this gift of a book.

**Alexandra Derwen, author of *Lost Rites: Ceremony
and Ritual for Death and Dying* and founder of
the Sacred Circle end of life doula preparation**

*The Birthkeeper of Bethlehem is a joyful paean to
the sacredness and power of women's wisdoms.*

Gina Martin, author of the *When She Wakes series*

A beguiling, well-crafted and emotion-packed tale. This book engages your heart and takes it on a wild, sometimes sensuous and evocative, ride. The Birthkeeper of Bethlehem has secured a place in the bookshelves of my heart's inner sanctum as a classic to return to again and again, such is its power and beauty.

Paula Cleary, Go With the Flow doula and birth activist

Supple weaves her love of Christ with her love of midwifery. If you want to know what it feels like to be a midwife in the home setting, read this book.

Gail Tully, creator of Spinning Babies® and author of *Changing Birth on Earth*

Bridget's writing casts the birth spell magically over me so I may enter the darkened room of women's work, with the primal smells of herbs, aromatic oils, honey, amniotic fluid, sweat, and love, as two stars in the sky draw mysteriously together.

Bridget Supple's word-medicine reminds me that we are all woven together, threads of many faiths, cultures, and traditions, mountains and oceans between us, yet we are but one swaddling cloth of humanity.

Bridget, thank you, for reminding me to take a heartbeat, gaze more often at the stars, walk home from birth in the rain, astonished by this blessed way of life, ancient and newborn.

Robin Lim, grandmother, midwife, founder of *Yayasan Bumi Sehat* (Healthy Mother Earth Foundation) health clinics, offering free prenatal care and birthing services in Indonesia. Author of *After the Baby's Birth, Wellness for Mothers, Ecology of Gentle Birth* and *Awakening Birth*.

The book sweeps you along, riding the waves of birth as though you are in the room with the women, holding the faith and celebrating when the baby is born. A wonderful story that could be read every Christmas time.

Nicola Mahdiyyah Goodall, traditional birth attendant

While the Christmas story is two thousand years old and is 'owned' by Christians and non-believers across the world, this book reclaims the intimacy and pathos of Christ's birth.

Bridget Supple is well qualified to write this story having spent twenty years as an antenatal teacher and tireless advocate for the rights of birthing women and families. Readers of faith and those of no faith will, I am sure, enjoy it as much as I did.

Mary Nolan, emerita professor of perinatal education, University of Worcester

I loved this book. Bridget's descriptions of the midwife's life, community, and settings are beautifully intricate and elicit wonderful vivid images in one's mind. I especially enjoyed the birth stories, waiting with baited breath as challenging births unfolded thanks to the midwife's wisdom.

Dr Sophie Messager, perinatal educator and author of *Why Postnatal Recovery Matters*

Bridget Supple weaves a beautiful tale of birth and midwives through this story about the birth of Jesus. She takes us into the birthing lives of the women of the region, whilst sharing the sacredness of the work of the midwife. A joy to read.

Mars Lord, Abuela Doulas

For the Birthkeepers

Prologue

Listening to the stories you could think He only surrounded himself with men. We seem to have become invisible. But we were there when He died, when the men – His friends, followers and Apostles – had fled for fear of the Romans. They hid. Not even there to see Him die, to lay out his cold, lifeless body. But I was there. Watching as the sky went dark and the life left Him. Just as I had been there when He was born and the sky lit up.

At the end, I helped His mother wash and wrap His broken, bruised and beaten body, in the same way as, thirty years earlier, we had washed and swaddled Him as a beautiful newborn baby.

I remember so clearly that night, when He was born in the company of women.

Nothing was the same after that.

Something as simple as the birth of a baby brought such pain and yet… So much change, so much love; such a remarkable time. Such a baby.

I was His midwife.

This is my story.

CHAPTER ONE

Talia

The rains are late. The town is dusty and crowded with people on the move as *Sukkot* is nearly upon us. Families are gathering from across the region ready to celebrate together, making the town unusually busy. Inns are full, shops increasing their prices as the market heaves with bodies. Sure, the traders do well, but those of us who live here are sharing our town with twice its normal numbers. The travellers bring new scents, much dust and excitement. Me, I enjoy it, although some around me grumble. Returning family and strangers all in their best and brightest making the streets come alive with colour; even my old eyes can feel the life in those patterns. Turbans and scarves, fancy jewellery, slaves, livestock so different to our own. My eyes are drawn to the energy rushing past: a flash of blue so striking it could be the sky, reds as deep as blood itself, so much colour and life.

Here, outside of the rainy season, all things are the colour of the desert dust. The roads, the buildings, the rocks are hewed from the same with only humans and flowers adding the paint to this dusty canvas. Every year when the rains come, the change is so complete it can take my breath away. Within two weeks of the rains that drench the soil – filling the roads and pouring in swirling gushes down buildings – the earth transforms itself. The desert blooms into a carpet of green and lush tones. Wildlife flourishes, flowers burst out in a flurry of joy, insects swarm. And then, within a few months, as if it was a careless mistake, the land dries up again; everything withers, dies and the soil returns to the familiar sandy hue, leaving only tiny pockets of plants.

It is the same with the travellers. While they are here, the area brightens as if a magical rug of bright threads has descended on the town. There is a friction and a joy at the same time. Travellers bring money, news and goods. They tell stories and fill the streets with chatter, bringing business and, occasionally, trouble. You feel the gaze of the old women in the doorways, watching with suspicious eyes from behind the door curtains. Children dart around together in joyful herds, chasing, playing and tumbling. The older ones gather in clusters to discuss all this life moving through their town. Here I sit, out of the heat of the day, but well-placed to watch the bustle. People greet me as they pass, "Shalom, Mother Salome!"

I see it all and I remember.

Every year, as the travellers come through, I am reminded of that year when Caesar Augustus forced thousands of people to travel across the land and back to their birthplaces to register. Not as we do today, to celebrate. Not for our benefit. No – simply so he could charge us for living. There were so many people on the move then as well: some passing through, some coming back, some leaving us for a long journey, a few never to return.

Soon my own house will be filled as my husband's brothers and their families all return to this, the family home. Some are arriving tonight and the rest over the next few days. My daughters are excited to be seeing their cousins, aunties and uncles again and I love having them with us. Just in case I am called to a birth, and with my daughters helping me, I am trying to get as much of the food preparation done as I can. My sisters-in-law are good women, they will help, but I need things ready just in case I am called out. The house is full of cured meats, bags of grains, spices and piles of fruit. Bundles of fresh herbs hang from the ceiling and fill the air with wafts of coriander, mint, parsley, fennel and chamomile, all releasing their scent as they are brushed against or blown by the wind.

My two girls and I are sitting together in the shady part of the courtyard. The sun climbs in the mid-morning sky, it is already hot in the direct sunshine. The high sandy walls that surround us protect us both from the world outside and the glare of heat. Plants creep up the worn rocks, dark leaves and red grapes hanging from the vines clinging to these weather-softened bricks.

Our hands are busy as we chop, spice and store the readied ingredients. To my left, sitting on the floor with her long legs stretched out is Shifra, my youngest daughter, her dark hair falling round her shoulders. It frames her face and shows her huge smile. She is laughing, shoulders shaking as we remember the last time the cousins came to visit, the jokes and fun they shared. Between her legs she has piles of dried herbs laid out on a cloth: thyme, oregano and sumac. A bag of toasted sesame seeds and a pot of salt help secure the cloth from the occasional gust of wind. She is stripping the herbs into a big wooden bowl, mixing them together to create the beautiful aroma of za'atar: a rich and so very familiar herb blend that I cannot ever smell without remembering cooking with my grandma.

On my right, on a small wooden stool, sits my elder daughter Martha, upright but relaxed. She is grinding a large bowl of cumin seeds ready to rub on the lamb that will slow cook in the courtyard oven. The heady fragrance overpowers all else for a moment, until the breeze blows it away. Martha, as always, laughs less than the joy-filled Shifra, but she chuckles softly, her kind face soft round the

4

edges, gentle and thoughtful like her father.

I'm also on a low stool, with a big bowl in front of me in which I'm swishing aubergines around in a swirl of water, clearing off any dirt with my hands, before I burn the skin off and stew them slowly. Over the years as a midwife I have learnt to make more of these meals that can cook long and slow: dishes that will not ruin if left in a warm oven overnight should I be called out. Preparing ahead whenever the opportunity presents is all part of being a birthkeeper. You never know when you might be called to a birth.

"Is that the door?" asks Shifra, stopping laughing and cocking her head to listen. "I think I can hear someone knocking."

Sure enough, there is a frantic knocking at the door. Drying my hands on a cloth tucked into my waistband as I rise, I cross our dusty courtyard and open the large wooden door onto the street. With apologies for disturbing us, a servant girl, sweaty and short of breath from running, asks me to attend her household.

"My mistress, Miriam, wife of Adam, sends me. Her daughter-in-law is in labour with her first baby. She is on the birthstool and has been pushing and pushing for so long but the baby does not come. She's getting very weak and we worry for her and the baby. Can you help?" her words are quick, falling over themselves to get out, her brow furrowed with concern.

I think I have seen Miriam at the temple, but I do not know her. I have not been their family's midwife before. It's really unusual for us not to know the mother before the birth. This is a small town. Ordinarily only about two hundred families fill our streets, so you see people grow up, grow old, live and die within a short walk of your doorstep. With some you know every intricacy of their lives and others you know just to greet, sometimes because you've not ever had the chance to get to know them and some because, well, you have. Many of the women whose births I attend I've known since they were babies, seen them grow or have attended the birth room for their mother, sister or aunts. I usually see a woman throughout her pregnancy, looking after her wellbeing, giving herbs for pregnancy discomforts, belly massages, helping to turn babies if needed, giving women nourishment and care as they go through this sacred time. They then know and trust me before we journey together through the wilderness of birth. A handful of families, however, have their own birthkeeper, or their births are attended by an older family member – perhaps that is why I was not aware of this pregnancy.

I begin to move quickly. If the mother is pushing, there is no time to waste. My second daughter, Shifra, jumps up excited to accompany me. As fast as she can, she runs her bundles of herbs and the za'atar mixture back to the shelter of the kitchen. "I'll get our bags ready," she calls as she dashes off, her excitement showing that birth is in her blood as much as mine.

Shifra is taller than me now with long and golden limbs. She's not yet troubled by the lines and flesh of age. Her whole self bounces with life and excitement, her quick eyes sparkle…delight, curiosity and shock all easy to see on her face. She has not yet learnt the filter and disguise that come with age. Her skirt, I notice, is starting to skim higher above her ankles after the last stretch of her bones. Those beautiful limbs formed in my own body, cradled, nourished, fed and held through childhood now stretched in this, the sunset of childhood.

Martha offers the servant girl a cooling drink while I hurry to help Shifra gather our things, feeling the urgency of the message. We are always ready. It is our trade, our livelihood, our love. Our basic kit is packed, we just need to add fresh items such herbs and bread. Saying goodbye to my husband, Benjamin, and leaving my eldest daughter Martha to continue the food preparation, we put on our sandals, grab our bags, cover our heads and step out, ushering the servant girl to show the way.

Weaving our way through the streets of Bethlehem, I can feel the stones pound my feet though my worn leather sandals. The hot air makes running hard work and very quickly sweat is trickling down my back. Occasionally, I feel the thud of arms bumping as we hurry through busy streets, I mutter apologies, but it's hard to avoid people in the narrower spaces. We scurry after the back of the servant girl, as she leads the way. She is faster than I am and every so often she glances back to check we are still following her.

Our route takes us through packed, narrow alleyways, where the houses are built so tightly together you could touch each other from your opposite doorsteps. We weave through the washing which is draped from window to window, displaying everyday life on each line, with splashes of reds and oranges, rich shades in sharp contrast to the pale ground beneath our feet and the walls around. We blend into the desert around us. Sometimes I think if you cut us through, our bones would be the same shade as these rocks, as if we are all made of these mountains.

We hurry past doorways with people sitting, talking, doing business, watching us rush. Passing thick curtains blocking entrances or closed ornate wooden doors. Stepping round life lived out on the pavements of this town...trading, cooking, meeting, greeting, praying. Life here is too crowded, and it is too hot, to keep it all indoors.

The servant girl dives around people, breaking into a sprint when the road gets less busy. I'm quite fit, but she has the advantage of youth and I cannot match her pace; however the urgency of the situation and the fear of being too late make me push to keep up with her. My lungs are burning hot, and I hold my birth bags tight like a baby across my chest. *Please let us be in time, please let us be in time,* runs through my head, a tightness gripping my chest that is not from the run but dread as the fear starts to rise. *God be with us,* I pray, *God be with this mother.*

The girl speeds even faster, knowing she is close to home. Her red headscarf bobs as she weaves down another alleyway. The smell of cooking, heat and humans packed together in this desert space overwhelms my already dizzy senses. I pant in the hot air and assure myself it's not much further.

Within a few minutes, we reach the house. We are in the finer area now, not the grand buildings occupied by the Roman rulers, but large, courtyard homes built into and onto the rocks that define and dominate this land. These are the houses where the owners are established and respectable. This house is as least three times the size of my own. I am impressed by its great solid walls, and huge front door, which as we approach, I can see is covered in beautiful intricate carvings. My husband Benjamin is a carpenter so I always appreciate fine craftsmanship when I see it and, even though worn through use, this door is magnificent. It opens as we get near, someone must have been watching and waiting for us.

As we enter, I reach to the upper right of the doorpost and touch an ornately decorated metal *mezuzah,* then kiss my fingers to my lips. The *mezuzah* is a small decorated box containing a scroll of parchment with passages from the Torah. It holds the word of God, and acts as the dividing line between the bustle of the outside world and the sanctity and safe haven of the home. Every Jewish home has one on the doorpost to offer protection to the home within. I love that you know where you are when you see it … we are with our people.

We are welcomed in, take off our shoes and wash our hands. Barely taking in our surroundings, we are hurried through the hallway into the cool of the building. Straight ahead of us are the living rooms and stairs up to the second floor and bedrooms. On top of them the rooftop, no doubt used for sleeping on those nights when there is no escape to be had from the heat. We go past the anxious faces of the household and through into the courtyard. Crossing the centre of this open space with its decorated well, a shady tree and bold tiles brightening the walls, we head to the left-hand side, stepping through a plain door into the women's quarters. The men of the household hold back, kept separate from this women's work.

After the heat of running, the courtyard is deliciously cool but, as we step into the birth room, a wall of heat hits, the result of oil lamps burning all night, combined with a room full of warm bodies. The taste of sweat, oil and heat combine in my throat as I breathe in this new air.

I look around the room. It is dark only because the shutters are closed. Its earthen walls have shelves built in. Oil lamps light the space casting dancing shadows and shapes. Bright rugs in red-hued patterns hang on two of the walls, adding warmth and life to the room. There are purple desert flowers in an earthenware jar in the nearest corner, losing the battle to cover the smell of heat and sweat. Next to it, an intricately carved wooden table on top of which sits a large brass tray with four goblets, a large jug filled with water and a scraggy fragrant wild mint that grows everywhere. There are also a selection of dates and fruits, snacks for the labouring mother and her supporters.

A rolled-up bed mat is placed neatly in another corner, alongside a large jug full of water for washing, with a bowl beside it on the pressed earth floor. On the back wall, lit by flickering oil lamps, there is a selection of wool on shelves with a loom, containing a half finished deep red rug, leaning up beneath. It is such a luxurious room for the women's space. While on our period or once in labour we enter a time when we must be separate from males. In our ancestors' time, in the desert, women would go to the red tent for their time of the month and for birth. When we settled in houses, a room or space was still set aside for this purpose, this is such a beautiful space to pass your blood-time – weaving, sewing, resting and talking with other women.

Helpful anxious hands take my bags to put them on a table. I'm passed a cooling drink of water. "Thank you, thank you for coming," I hear as I'm handed the goblet and quickly quench my thirst after the run.

Gradually, I see her as my eyes adjust to the dark...the labouring mother is in the furthest corner. I am told as I approach her that her name is Talia.

Surrounded by the women of her family, she is on the stone birth-stool. In our pack we carry birthstones but here they are not needed as the house has this carved birthing chair. The same stones that make the walls, road and ground have been chiselled into the shape of a crescent moon so the mother can be open and upright during the birth. Birthstools stay in a family and generations of women will birth on them, reminding each mother of the women who have gone through this before her. They allow a woman to conserve her energy as she births, while her being upright assists the baby's descent.

But this birthing mother is so tired she is struggling to hold herself up even while on the stool. Green fluid dribbles down her legs like muddied river water, as she sits swaying and moaning, face creased in pain. Stepping close, I cause her to open her eyes by gently placing my hand on her arm. As I do, I notice the red thread tied around her wrist for protection, just as I have one on mine. They are often given by mothers to their children but especially to women for childbirth. Made of plaited wool they are dyed with the *shani*, the tiny bugs found on oak trees. I notice all the women in the room have one on, they are all joined with her as she births this baby.

"Hello Talia, I am Salome, I am here to help you."

I crouch down and gently put my hands on her feet, softly cupping the tops, holding and transmitting connection. It is such a simple gesture, but it always seems to help ground a mother who is drifting. Perhaps it prompts her to feel her feet touching the earth, maybe it reminds her of where she begins and ends. I do not know, but I know it is always a help. It also allows me to feel her legs. It's one of many things my mother taught me: as a woman gets more dilated, her lower legs get colder, the cold rising from the feet to the knees.

"Feel her calves," she would say, getting me to feel the legs of a labouring woman. "If she is cold only in the lower part, you have plenty of time. If she is cold as high as her knees, though, she is usually fully dilated. See, Salome, there are so many signs to help us observe the course of labour, if you just know where to look."

Talia's feet and calves feel cold. Her eyes open and look for mine. Large, walnut-coloured eyes, quite startling in their size, look tired and she finds it hard to focus. Then she finds me...we connect. By now, Shifra is by my side, whispering what she has already found out in my ear, her voice still out of breath from the run.

"Green waters...broke hours ago. She's been in labour since yesterday. The women tell me she's been very scared by this birth and they have been trying to keep her calm but the pain has overwhelmed her." She leans back towards me, "Oh, and the contractions have been irregular since the start."

I love my daughter; she has gone straight to work finding out what we need to know. She has learnt from me, just as I learnt about birth from my mother and she from her mother before her. I feel the women in my family have been midwives forever. I feel the knowledge in my bones. The labour started a day and night ago, tightenings without a pattern and they had continued strong but never becoming regular. Immediately, I get that feeling in my stomach, when you just know. An irregular pattern means one thing. Always. This is a breech or differently positioned baby. Time after time, an irregular pattern of contractions has indicated a baby arriving feet or bottom first, or warned us that the baby is starting its arrival facing the mother's front and to prepare for a longer labour. It is a signal to rest more in the early stages, then later, a warning to make the space for that baby.

Time does strange things in a birth room. Hours can fly in a moment and a moment take an age, but Talia's mother-in-law, Miriam, whose house this is, speaks up and confirms this has now taken a long time. Her voice is heavy with concern. "She's been pushing since the early hours of the morning. It's too long and the baby is not to be seen."

I'm surprised I was not called earlier. I pray again I am not too late.

Miriam is a strong, handsomely featured woman with presence in her every move. She becomes increasingly beside herself. "I should have called you earlier," she says, grasping my arm. "Our Dodah has delivered all the babies born in this house, but she is so old now and I fear she is forgetting her skills."

She looks over at an ancient-looking, petite woman with translucent skin who is clearly upset that I have been brought here.

Miriam, looking anguished, whispers in my ear, "She used to be so sharp, but recently her whole personality has changed – she doesn't always know who we are. I wanted to call someone else, but my husband insisted she was the family midwife." Miriam's voice drops even quieter as she adds, "When I went out and told him we might lose our grandchild, he let me call you."

I look at the Dodah. Her face is lovely, but she is so very old and frail. Perhaps she has reached that stage where she is forgetting herself and gradually shedding her memories and her life as she readies herself to meet her maker. Not many, but some of our elders walk this path before we lose them. It makes the leaving easier for them as they forget all they cared for in this life, but it is so much harder for those being left behind. I know now that is why they did not call sooner: it was Dodah's job. Still, I am here now and I must see whether or not I am too late.

I watch Talia have a contraction and feel her belly while she has it. As the contraction comes, I see the uterus push out and feel her tummy harden. Good, the contractions are still strong, even if the mother has weakened. I watch the next one: they are still coming, but Talia can barely hold herself upright for each. As they come, she cries out and pushes, her back arching and legs tensing. I crouch down, head under the birthstool to see if the baby is there as she pushes but there is no sign of any descent.

I need to know what is happening. I look Talia in the eyes and say, "I need to find out why baby is not coming." Talia looks scared. "Shhh, there, there," I say. "I'm here for you. Now, I know this is hard but I'm going to ask you to let me feel where the baby is."

She nods her head, flopping forward, hair wet with sweat and sticking to her glistening skin. Her bare belly hangs forward, legs opened by the birthing stool.

A woman brings me a bowl of water and a cloth. I clean and wipe my hands, then Shifra pours almond oil on to make my hands soft. We mutter the blessings on my hands, performing the rituals, in the hope that God will spare this mother and baby. I do not ask Talia to change position. I will see if I can do it without disturbing her first. My mother could feel the position of a baby in a minute. She never needed a woman to lie down to feel, her fingers were so practiced and so skilled. If the mother was lying down, it was much easier; but she taught me to feel whatever position a woman was in, so as not to disturb the birthing flow.

I feel her tummy first, my hands starting up at the top of her belly, fingers feeling, pushing, moving – *is that the bottom? Is that the head?* Moving right down the sides, my fingers exploring between tightenings. Down to her pelvis, her soft brown skin stretched tight around her protruding bump, again my fingers feeling for shape, outlining the belly. I close my eyes and breathe, slowly mapping the baby in my head. I think it is coming bottom first: the irregular contractions, the muddied water, the lack of descent when she pushes combined with what I've just felt build a picture. These all suggest that this is the reason this labour is not progressing as expected.

I ask her to let me feel inside. She looks scared, but her mother-in-law, Miriam, nods and rushes to reassure her. She positions herself to the side of Talia and cradles her head, stroking her hair and muttering soothing words. I pour more oil onto my fingers and lie on the floor underneath her. Wherever the baby is, the midwife needs to be underneath. It is rarely glamorous or comfortable. The air is cooler down here after the heat of the lamps. I feel the earth under me, grounding me, but there is no time to enjoy this sensation. Reaching in through the gap made by the birthing stool, I gently insert two fingers. I don't have to reach far, *what is that? Yes...a bottom!*

I'm almost relieved, the baby is not lying sideways or unable to descend, but we are not safe yet. If she has been labouring a long time, the baby may be dead already... I cannot tell. Shifra catches my eye, knowing what I am about to say, her knowledge and confidence in her ability growing every year. I sit up and wipe my hands and in a low reassuring voice explain to Talia, "Your baby is coming bottom first. Do not worry, I know how to help but you must listen to me and do as I say."

Talia groans and nods. The room is suddenly deathly quiet, everyone holding their breath as the realisation dawns that things are at a fork, a moment that might change the outcome.

We need to get her off the birthstool, it will not help a baby coming bottom first. She needs to be on her hands and knees, but she is flopping with tiredness. "I need you to get off the birthstool and onto your knees, we will help you." Then turning to the women in the room "Quick," I add, "she needs honey water."

The women in the room snap out of their collective breath-hold. There is movement in the dark as someone goes to the small table and fills a goblet with water. Honey and mint are added and this nectar for birthing mothers is mixed – the honey melts quickly in the warm water. It will give her energy and a lift.

Miriam and I start to help her off the stool and onto her hands and knees, turning her round so Shifra and I can be behind her ready for the baby. Miriam takes her place on the birthstool so she can be close to Talia's head to offer support and encouragement. In an all fours position with her full belly now weighing heavily toward the ground, the best space can be made in the pelvis, allowing this baby to navigate it's way down bottom first. Fresh sand to soak up the dribbling waters is put underneath her by a birdlike woman with soft olive arms wrapped in silver jewellery. The contractions keep coming. Talia moans with each one. She's hard to talk to as she's so distracted by the exhaustion and pain of each contraction. Between each tightening sensation we support and encourage her.

I hope and pray to myself that moving her will have given the baby the space it needs. Watching from as early as I can remember, I'd seen my mother turn those with bottom-first babies on to their fronts, leaning over chairs, beds, shaky arms holding their weight.

"Make space, Salome," she would say. "When the bottom comes before the head, it is you who must use your head and think about how to give the baby as much room as you can."

The room has gone very quiet. All the women are watching me, I can see the worry in their eyes. In the new stillness we can hear the sound of the men reciting psalms outside. Their job, in labour, is to pray the specific passages for mother and baby. We are in a separate woman's world that they cannot enter.

"May God answer you in your day of trouble,
May the name of the God of Jacob place you in safe shelter."

I suddenly feel the heat in the room again, feeling the pressure of all this hope, this family, this woman, this baby. It makes me feel clammy for a moment, but I have had this situation before and this feeling before and I remind myself with a quiet prayer that I can only do my best and I *will* do my best.

Another contraction is coming. Talia starts to cry out, but at the same time she is pushing. Moving her from the stool has done something, perhaps given the baby space where it had none. Shifra is at her side in a moment. Together we encourage, support and soothe her.

Another contraction and I crouch low to the floor, looking up to check progress. Her bottom is flared wide, a purple line high up its crack, showing she has dilated fully, "There are so many signs a baby is coming, Salome." I remember my mother's instruction, "Look for the line." The birthline is a purple-hued line rising in the gap between the bottom cheeks. The longer the line, the more dilated she is. In some women it is obvious, and in some, it is trickier to spot, but when visible it can help you see how far she has to go.

As she pushes, I can see the baby's bottom start to move down. This is good. "Your baby is coming. With the next contraction I need you to open your legs and help it down. Do what your body wants to do," I say.

The contraction finishes and we offer Talia honey water while Shifra mops her brow, stroking her sweaty hair out of the way as you would a child's. We do not touch her belly or buttocks any more. Now we know the baby comes breech, nothing should be done to cause the mother to flinch. Breech births are a balance of hands-off and readiness to help if needed.

The women in the room talk in hushed voices. The woman with the wrinkled hands is now holding the hands of a young cousin of the father. She's only a girl and, I suspect, she has only just started her bloodtime. But now, as a woman in the house, she is here at the birth, watching and learning, so that when she herself gives birth it will not be an unknown. She grips the elderly woman's fragile hands tightly, face set in fear. All eyes are on us. Most have seen births. They have seen the joy, pain and delight of a new life. However, some have also seen a mother bleed to death, or a baby born lifeless and grey. A new baby is to be celebrated, but birth is still to be feared, it is known here as one foot in the grave time.

Miriam stays close to Talia's head, stroking her hair, hands providing comfort even though her face is etched with worry. Another contraction starts. Talia roars, the voice of women throughout the ages as they create life and force a baby through to the living world. Again, I crouch and see her opening as the bottom descends. She is stretching open, the burning sensation making her cry out.

The minute it lasts is long and, as the contraction ends, Talia sinks down. We offer more comfort and sweet drink. I give her a minute then ask her to raise one leg, as I remember my mother's voice saying, "Make space." Breech babies, above all, need space. It might be kneeling or moving the knees closer together that changes the space the baby has to make use of. Space and the advantage of being upright are crucial when the baby is coming into the world bottom first.

"Talia, I need you to listen to me. I need you to put one leg out to the side. We need to give this baby more room. Can you do that? We will help you."

Talia nods but does not let it interrupt her long breath and she lifts her right knee forward into a raised kneel. Another contraction begins and she pushes again. We give no more instruction, letting her listen to what her body wants to do. The noise she makes is so powerful that I hear the men outside stop their prayers momentarily in fear, then continue faster and more intently. This powerful sound moves the baby down, the bottom showing outside as another trickle of green water runs down to the floor. As the contraction ends, the bottom is visible. Another rest, these small gaps making the pain bearable. I remember my mother reassuring first time mothers with her gentle voice whispering, "It is not a constant pain. It comes and goes like waves on a shore – each time pulling back and leaving you for a few minutes before the next one."

As Talia roars through the next contraction, the bottom crowns and the top of the legs become visible. Blue skin alarms me, but I know it's not uncommon in a breech birth. The legs start to emerge until, slipping and slithering, they flop down to a shout of pain from Talia. Now the baby's head is inside and the body hangs down outside her. Even with all my skills, even with all of my years of experience, my instinct is to reach out, but you are best not to touch unless needed. It's the weight of the baby that helps the next stage of the birth, ideally you will just let it happen and only intervene if necessary.

"Sit on your hands, if you cannot trust them," my mother would say. It is not long before the next contraction, but it feels like an eternity. I notice the body with elongated legs dangling down, and a small penis tucked in between the legs. It is a boy, a blessing for the family but, me, I loved my daughters more than the world.

The baby's body is bluish. I strain in the lamp lit room to see signs of a heart beating, movement. *Please God, spare this child. Please God, let him live* runs through my head. Talia is dangerously close to giving up.

"Your baby is nearly here," we tell her. She is crying in pain. Hot tears mingle with the sweat pouring down her face. "Now listen, Talia, don't push again until you feel the contraction and then let's get this baby out, your son."

At the words 'your son' she stops crying. Our eyes meet.

"Really? A son?"

"Yes. Now you are so close, let's meet him," I reply.

I've seen the magic work before on a mother who cannot push anymore, who cries out in pain. For a mother with a headfirst baby, if you can get her to touch her baby's head, to feel it between her legs, it will be transformative. She gets it: she actually believes it's working and will push her baby out. To Talia, the news it is a boy has the same effect. She locks eyes with me. I whisper encouragement, praise. I promise it is nearly over and she pushes hard, filling the room with her cry.

The cry of a mother birthing could chill a soul. It is pain and love and power all together. It is the strongest and most vulnerable sound you will ever hear. Talia roars and her cry is felt by all the women in the room. It links her with us, with the women who birthed before her, with all the women who have birthed throughout time. We are women. We birth. We roar.

I return my concentration to the baby, dangling between her legs. As she bears down the head is not descending. I can see the head is extended up. It cannot come out. The extension means the chin is too high, it should be tucked on the chest, making the head smaller. Lifted up it makes the head awkward to deliver. The baby is stuck. My heart sinks and a chill strikes me.

Time is now of the essence. If the baby dangles too long there is a chance the cord will be compressed and the infant may die. I lean into Shifra, who I think has realised the danger too. "I need to help the head," I say to her. "Can you get Talia ready?" and she nods a quick, tense acknowledgment. She knows that we have to move fast to keep this baby alive.

Shifra moves close to Talia's face and says, as reassuringly as she can, "Salome will assist the baby's head. This may hurt."

As the contraction continues, Talia pushes hard, gasping and groaning. My fingers are already slick with oil and carefully, so carefully, I slide my middle finger up to the baby's mouth to carefully pull down on the chin. With my thumb, I push softly at the back of the baby's head, pushing the chin towards the chest. Talia screams in pain but his head flexes forwards and the chin becomes visible. I remove my hands and as Talia pushes with all her might, he slips out into my hands, muddy water following in a gush.

I turn him over, cord still attached. He's limp. He's making no sound and there is a blue hue over his open-mouthed face. Immediately I lay him down on the floor between Talia's legs and rub his chest. The room is silent. The women can see something is not right. Talia, exhausted after the exertion, has buried her head into Miriam's belly not yet realising how serious the situation is. Still he does not breathe. Again I rub this tiny blue chest, willing him to gasp a breath. Bending down, I cover his lips with mine, blowing into his mouth then turn back to rubbing his chest. Shifra is by my side, all eyes now on the lifeless baby. I'm muttering to him, "Breathe, breathe!" as I rub his slippery new skin, still wet from the birth canal.

Every fibre of my body wills him to splutter into life. I quickly lift him and turn him onto his front. His lifeless body hangs over my hand as I tilt him to allow any fluid to dribble out of his mouth. Then I rotate him over onto his back to rub his chest again.

Talia has realised something is wrong and, with growing panic, she starts to scream, but all my attention has to be on the baby. I can see the movement of the other women rushing to reassure her and keep her where she is as I work. I'm just focused on the little one, willing him to live as I rub and breathe into him in turn.

I glance down at the umbilical cord, still attached between him and his mother. It had been compressed in the last moments of the birth – how long for I do not know, but I see that its pulsation, so slow immediately after the birth, is now looking healthier. I rub his chest and give one more breath to his tiny, still mouth…I'm just reaching to his chest to rub again when suddenly he coughs and splutters, and then cries. He's breathing!

The room erupts. I realise I'm shaking. I watch him for a moment, rub him down with a cloth and pass him between Talia's legs as she turns over to lay him on her chest. Cushions appear behind her. The gathered women are kissing and stroking her and hugging each other in relief and joy. News has been passed outside or the sound of the baby crying must have been heard. We hear the cheer and celebrations of the men, then sounds of prayers being sung in the courtyard outside this women's space.

Shifra and I, however, know we are not safe yet. A difficult birth can often cause a reluctant placenta. Women can bleed to death after a complicated birth – our work is not yet finished. We watch the baby closely while all the time checking the blood loss from under Talia. Old cloths are laid out underneath her to mop up the trickling blood – and now we wait. Shifra is getting the cords out of our bag to bind the umbilical cord before we cut it. We always wait though to cut until after the placenta has been delivered.

We offer Talia a sip from a small goatskin bag. It is wine, with raspberry leaf, honey and chamomile, to ease her pain, restore her energy, calm her down and, most importantly, help her deliver the placenta. She sips a small mouthful while still hugging her baby. Her long black hair sticks to her sweat soaked skin. There is a strange beauty to a woman just after birth. The stress and strain of birth disappear from her face, her skin fills and she looks otherworldly. She has survived. She has felt this incredible pain but birthed her baby. She has realised the amazing strength of her body and brought a life forth from it.

I keep a watchful eye on the baby, cradled on his mother's chest, his skin returning to a normal shade. He is moving and occasionally lets out a small cry as the women in the room stroke his head and deliver big kisses in turns. There is so much love for this mother and baby.

I would not expect a placenta to follow immediately after a breech birth but I know that every minute counts. After a straightforward birth, a delay is less of a concern but after a delayed breech I'll worry until it is out and checked. I have a gentle feel of her belly, a second baby might now show itself, but it feels empty. Talia has another sip from our goatskin bag and strokes the little one's head. We sit next to

21

her, watching the baby snuggle and start to root for the breast. Even after that difficult start its drive to survive is inbuilt.

I watch the cord. It is still pulsating, still working hard for the baby. Gradually, it starts to turn a paler colour and the rhythmical beat slows. It always feels like watching life ebb away now it has finished the task of bringing the baby to the world: the original connection between the baby and mother finally finishing its job. There, it has stopped. Hopefully the placenta will follow soon. Breastfeeding usually helps it along.

On the floor there is a tightly woven reed basket lined with scraps of wool ready to catch the placenta, which, once delivered, will need to be checked, prepared and buried today. After what seems like an age, a small gush of blood appears between Talia's legs: a good sign that the placenta is on its way. "I feel fullness down there," she says with a puzzled look.

"It's the placenta coming," I reassure her. "Kneel up to help it out." Holding her baby close, she crawls onto her knees. We hold the basket underneath her as with a small push the placenta plops out. Now the cord can be cut. We bring the basket close to her and Miriam helps tie the cord in two places with two tightly plaited wool strips. "As tight as you can!" I remind her.

Once they are tied, our small, sharp dagger with its wooden handle encrusted with mother of pearl is used by Miriam to cut the cord. First it is heated in the flame of the oil lamp and then I hold the cord firm as she cuts between the wool bindings. All the women clap and hug to celebrate this significant step in the new baby's life. The act symbolises the start of the baby's life on its own.

The placenta sits in the basket, blood already seeping through the tiny gaps. I pick it up and lay it out on a small piece of reed matting, which afterwards will be burnt, to check it is all there. It is warm still and cups around my hands as I stretch it out, ensuring that no parts of it remain inside Talia. It looks healthy and, most importantly, complete. I thank it for its work before an aunt takes it to prepare it for burial.

We stay with Talia for many hours after the birth, checking her bleeding and ensuring feeding is going well. We do not really need to help with the baby, as there are so many pairs of hands to lovingly wash him with oil and salt, provided with a flourish by a very proud Miriam, now glowing with pride and delight. She had waited for this moment since her own last son was born. The new baby is lovingly washed and swaddled, while prayers and celebrations are whispered in his ears as the women stroke and love him. Such a welcome baby.

The whole household is alive with joy, celebrating the birth. A feast is being prepared and thanks given to Yahweh for this son. The boy had been taken out and presented to his father and the men of the household and then returned to his mother in this womb-like birth space. The bed mat in a deep red woven fabric stuffed with wool and camel hair is rolled out on the floor for Talia and the baby, patterned cushions surround her head. There are old rags underneath her to catch the blood and a sacred amulet that had been above the birthstool during labour, is now hung above the bed to protect her from Lilith. Lilith, the banished first wife of Adam who seeks her revenge by killing newborns. The amulet, a palm sized carving of the three protective angels, Sanvei, Sansenvei and Semangel, depicted as three figures with the heads of cocks along with their written names will stay with Talia while she is in confinement.

Talia lies down and Miriam brushes her hair as gently as if she were a child. An aunt wearing a long dark dress with swirling orange embroidery at the cuffs and hem washes away the dried blood on her legs and gently rubs sweet fragrant oils into her soft brown skin making the space smell refreshed and flowery. Another, a middle-aged elegant woman with a long, lined face framed by silver-speckled black hair, washes her arms and chest, cleaning away the sweat. There will be a proper ritual cleansing later, but for now it is just to make her comfortable and ease her exhausted body.

The women move as smoothly as a hive of bees, all working towards the common purpose of caring for this newly birthed mother. The buzz of activity is orchestrated by Miriam. It is a wonderful sight. Songs and prayers can be heard from the rest of the house. The mood is joyful and light after the fear of the birth. I sit with Miriam as we watch over Talia and the baby. We are offered food and drink, and as often happens in the sacred space around a birth, stories are told and hearts are opened. Miriam glows with love for this new baby and I remark how lovely it is to see a woman care so tenderly for a daughter that is not hers. She laughs, "How easy it is to love such a beautiful hearted girl who has made my son so happy and made me a grandmother." Then her face takes a more serious look.

"My sister was so like her: beautiful, warm, just so loveable. We were the best of friends. But when she married, her mother-in-law was a horrible woman, cold-hearted and mean. She only cared for her son and my beautiful sister could not do right. Even when she bore them sons, her mother-in-law was not happy. She constantly pushed my sister out, and treated her harshly in front of the boys. There were so many years of meanness and control until it crushed her very spirit."

She pauses, the emotions shaking out of her, tears in her eyes, "You see it in the boys. They are my nephews and of course I love them, but they are weak and poorly in body and spirit. Without a strong loved mother, they could not thrive. When I married, my mother-in-law Elizabeth was so kind. She loved me like a daughter and I swore I would do the same." She laughs her playful, deep laugh, "And so now I have the daughter I never bore, and am so, so lucky. My grandchild will have a strong and well-loved mother to love him and bring him up well."

I like Miriam. It is true. When women are treated badly at home, everyone is worse off for it. I see it when women are beaten at home, the babies are jittery, the whole house tense, and the boy children often grow up to be bullies themselves. Too often the daughter-in-law is just used as a slave, to cook, clean and bear children, which the grandmother then takes as her own. I have never seen the children grow up well when that happens: it's like a poison that seeps through the generations. Cruelty and unkindness take hold, grow and eventually reap a bitter crop.

Only when we are sure that Talia is safe do we gather our things. With a promise to return tomorrow to check on her, we leave this laughing, smiling throng of women, all of whom hug and kiss us, so grateful we had arrived when we did. They had seen Death lurking in the room and felt the cold hand of Chance hovering over the baby.

As we make our way to the door, leaving this warm dark womb-like space still pungent with the smell of birth and sweat, a bag of coins and a bottle of fragranced oil wrapped in brightly coloured cloth is pressed into my hand, accompanied by more kisses. Miriam, bursting with the pride of a first-time grandmother, has ensured we are well rewarded. Her strong features are dominated by a huge smile that has not left since the moment the baby took a breath: her first grandson, from her first-born son. Our knowledge feels like a gift, but it is our livelihood and without payment we would have to do other work. Then those skills would be lost. We would not be there, babies would be lost, mothers would die. I am grateful for the birth knowledge my mother gave me, but I am also thankful to be paid and know that we will be called back for every future birth in this house.

We exit the heat of the women's room and step into the cool of the courtyard, drinking in the fresh air and the sight of the sky. The sun is setting and the stars begin to appear. The courtyard, that I had hurried through with such fear in my heart earlier, now feels deliciously cool having been shaded all day by the large fig tree in the middle.

The courtyard sits in a square in the centre of the house. The walls are built of the pale rock from which all Bethlehem buildings are made, creating a light space, while at the same time providing shelter from the glare of the sun. There are pots in the corners and painted doors to the rooms that encircle this oasis at the core of the house. A small walkway provides a protected passageway and shade for the rooms. It is tastefully decorated but not showy, and demonstrates a real love for simple beauty. In the west corner there is the family well. These large houses often have their own well within the courtyard – the poorer you are, the further you have to go for your water. Its presence has allowed them to grow such a large tree, dripping with succulent fruit, creating a sanctuary during the summer from the merciless heat.

We are met with more thanks, this time from the gathered men. A huge man with a perfect full black beard steps forward. It is Adam, Miriam's husband, the new grandfather. He's tall and strong, wearing a fine quality robe made of cream cotton, his deep black hair joining an equally deep black beard. He has laughter lines around his eyes and is grinning from ear to ear.

"Thank you! Thank you!" he booms. Turning to face the other men he introduces us as if we are of great importance, "My friends, this is Salome and Shifra. Masters of their craft and friends of this family."

Birth opens up souls like you would not believe. We midwives become etched onto the story of a family and very often even if we forget them, they do not forget us. Adam turns and looking at us each in turn says quietly and solemnly, "You have saved my grandson. You are now family. I thank you from the bottom of my heart." Turning again he broadcasts to the entire courtyard, "These women are always welcome in my home and shall be with us for all future babies!" Everyone cheers as the joy and relief after the stress bubbles out of the gathered men.

The new father, Uri, who has not stopped smiling, has his hair ruf-

26

fled and back patted by the group of joyful men as he steps forward with a blush and laughs. "Another baby, Father? After all that! I can't go through that again!" he says, feigning drama.

The men roar with laughter and Adam, quick as flash, replies, "Now your mother has a taste for being a grandmother, she won't be disappointed you know!" and hugs his son like a bear to the sound of laughter from the celebrating men.

I think the party will last for days in this house, the joy is so absolute. It takes us an age to cross the courtyard to the door, as we are introduced to uncles, friends and brothers. Adam offers us a cart ride, but we both agree that we need the walk and thanking him, head off.

We haven't had a chance to talk much to each other in the birth room. It was busy and there was so much chatter. This is our time to decompress and exchange thoughts.

"I am worn out," says Shifra, stretching a yawn as we walk, "...and that was a quick birth."

It is true. We were not even there a night and a day, as we often are for a first labour. Births are physically, emotionally and spiritually draining if you are properly present. I remark that my mother always said that you could tell those who were not true birthworkers as they did not invest in a woman or her baby, they saw it as just a process. "The process of birth, your grandmother would say, is an opening to a closeness with God that you get at no other time. It is a reminder of how God formed each one of us in love and work. It is such a powerful, spiritual event and not to be treated lightly."

I pick up where my mother's words left off, "To be truly present at birth is to remember this. It is too easy to treat it as 'just another birth'. To forget that is to forget that this is an experience that will forge and change a mother, that it is a spiritual and not just a physical event. If you treat it as only a process, you have forgotten it is a holy moment. That God is entrusting a child to the world, to this woman, and we should receive them with love and reverence for this gift."

Shifra is quieter than normal as we walk home. She's been attending births with me since she was around six, when she sat with wide-eyed wonder at the scene in front of her. She is now fifteen and will soon be married and gone. My heart cannot even think of the day she will not be by my side. Eventually she punctures the silence.

"I thought we had lost him. He was so blue when he came out. I felt sick. I could not breathe with fear." Her pace slows as she looks at the ground. "What if we had lost him, Mama? How did you stay so calm?"

I slow my pace to match hers and hold her hand.

"I did not know if he would live. I too thought that he might be dead and I was scared. Birth is scary sometimes. Often, actually. But we are not the ones who decide which babies live. That is in God's hands. Remember, God gave us these hands and this knowledge to help, to do our best. You must always try to be brave, even if you feel terrified. The mothers need us to be brave. Whatever the outcome, you must know that you tried your best."

I pause and turn to look her in the eyes. Her brown eyes that have the slightest tinge of yellow around the centre, making them striking against her dark skin.

"You will lose babies, my love. They will be born still or die in early life. It is the most terrible pain for all who experience it, but it is part of our work. You cannot shy away from it. You have to find a way to love those women and babies even more. As midwives, we are the ones who welcome these souls to the world, but we are also their first defence against Death. Death is always attracted when new life is close. You will feel him circling, waiting, hopeful. We must do what we can, but know that if God has decided a baby is to be with Him, all our skills will not help." Shifra nods and squeezes my hand.

I stop there, but inside there is so much more I want to tell her. At birth you walk with life and death in the room, with fear and elation, waiting to see on which side the coin will land. That's why secrets are often revealed in the birth room – it's an opening in so many ways. For labouring women it is a raw, physical, rebuilding experience. She, and she alone, has to face the physicality of her body, to find a way to trust that she will survive and this baby can come out of her. We are there to support her, to use our wisdom and knowledge, but she has to walk the path.

As we slowly make our way home, clutching my bag to my chest. I try to find the words I need for Shifra, "You can see it. The rawness of birth strips everything away. It can be frightening when a woman is labouring naked, and not caring, roaring with a voice that she has never heard before, feeling the power of her body to produce and bring forth life. It will change her forever. Like Moses in the desert, she must walk her path, trust God, and find her truth. It is our secret. There is a strength that lies in all women, especially if they are supported and shown love. It can be transformative. But when a woman is not supported in her labour, it can break her."

"That's why what we do is so sacred," I continue, "I think that in that moment of vulnerability and power, women need women around them who will honour and love them. When that is present, in that moment of magic, you birth a strong mother as well as a strong baby. The job of those around her – our job – is to support her, encourage and help her." Then I laugh, "And a bit of your grandmother's wisdom helps too."

Shifra leans in and rests her head on my shoulder. We are both feeling a strange mixture of exhaustion and at the same time, fully alive.

It is getting dark and we are nearly home. Up above, the stars sparkle, the sky is clear and the conjoining stars, the ones that are causing such a stir, look as if they are just about to touch in a heavenly embrace.

CHAPTER TWO

Bethlehem

We return home, clean up, and repack our bags. Sometimes it's hard to sleep after a birth, there is too much excitement coursing through the body. By the time we have finished and I have reached the point of sleepiness, it is past midnight. My husband Benjamin is already asleep – his gentle snores soothing in the dark. In the still of the night, I say goodnight to the stars, thank God for the care of Talia and fall fast asleep.

Dawn comes with the sounds of cocks crowing, dogs barking and heat rising. The morning passes cheerfully with food preparation, pregnancy and post-birth visits by the three of us. Martha, my eldest daughter, is going to visit a new mother whose birth she attended with me a week before.

The first weeks after a birth are a sacred and dangerous time. Women are raw and vulnerable and great harm can come to them if they are not well cared for. For forty days, a new mother is not to perform any task, care for older children or prepare any food. Every day there are healing rituals to be performed, these will usually be done by a female family member, but where help is scarce, we will go daily to attend the mother in this special, sacred time. Her belly will be massaged with beautiful infused oil, mustard for warming, perhaps lavender or chamomile for soothing. Then the postnatal belly will be bound tight with cloths to help restore her balance and return her health. It is our way to feed women warming, nourishing foods and drinks every day, taking care of the new mother while she supports this new fledgling life.

Shifra has returned to the house of Miriam to check on Talia's blood loss, though with so many female members of her household to care for her, we might not be required to perform the daily rituals.

From mid-morning our courtyard is filled with a steady flow of pregnant women and those hoping to become pregnant. After the birth, in the forty days, we go to them, but during pregnancy they come to me, perhaps popping in on their way to or from town. It means my small courtyard is regularly filled with the sound of children as they run around and play with the wooden toys Benjamin has made – balls and a selection of tiny animals, beautifully carved and smoothed by the hands of so many children. Our house is not large, but we are very blessed to have space enough for us all.

The house was built by Benjamin, his brothers and father. Before their death, Benjamin's parents had lived here with us, which had been both lovely and challenging. Benjamin's mother, Yoana, had never approved of me working, especially not after I had the girls. She believed, very strongly and vocally, that a woman should look after the home and children only. Often I had to bite my tongue or let Benjamin defend me in his quiet way. I would hear them having discussions if I missed meals she'd prepared or wasn't there to prepare them when it was my turn. For Benjamin, my not practicing midwifery was never in question. He knew when he fell in love with me that this is who I am, just as much as the body I inhabit.

They were difficult years. When I arrived as Benjamin's wife she expected me to give it all up for the running of the household. When his younger brothers married, their wives did just that, making it hard for me not to be seen as the uncooperative one. His father,

Baruch, however, was on my side. A gentle understanding soul, I could see where my husband's personality was formed and I'd often catch him standing out of sight of his wife, signalling to me to not mind the telling off.

It took years for Yoana to get it. It wasn't until her daughters-in-law started having babies and I took care of them that she saw that this was a useful vocation. Gradually, she would begrudgingly be proud when people thanked her for my role in their or their family member's birth. While I loved her in many ways, she sometimes made the eleven years of a shared household hard going.

As the eldest, the house had passed to Benjamin when they died. Each of the three brothers and two sisters had called this home at one point, but gradually most had moved for work or marriage. Only Eitan, Benjamin's youngest brother, had stayed in Bethlehem. He and his family lived here with us, bringing great joy and helpful hands, as well as a partner in work for Benjamin.

The layout of our house is typical of the area. You enter through our intricately carved front door, made by Benjamin, he reflected in it the tree he works with the most: the olive tree. Each panel of the door is a testament to his craftsmanship, with the detailed patterns and form of an olive tree throughout. Through the door you come straight into a small courtyard with rooms around the edge. On the left, at the front of the house, is Benjamin's workshop, which has a separate door onto the street for customers. It has a small entry to the courtyard, so while I have women here, he closes a heavy curtain.

On the back wall of the courtyard there is the entrance to two small sleeping rooms, one for Benjamin and me, and one for Eitan and

Hadar and their baby. On the right is a living space with a large chest that doubles as a table. The girls sleep together in a room at the back. The flat roof is used for extra space, weaving and occasionally sleeping.

Hadar is here helping me today. With her baby strapped on her back, she is tending the fire and cooking the stew we will feed the mothers. It's customary to offer food to all who come and especially important as some mothers either do not have enough at home or perhaps are never cared for. I make it a point to offer everyone a bowl of nutritious stew made of barley, beans, lentils, dates, cabbage, nettles, onions, garlic and herbs, whatever I have to spare or have been given. Our pot bubbles on a low heat all morning, ensuring that the women in my care are made healthier, stronger and ready for birth.

First in this morning is Denah, who has been struggling to get pregnant. She has already been married for a year. A plain, but kind girl, I have known her all her life – I had been there when she was born into the hands of my mother. She worked hard in her home and had married Gil, a young man from the town, who worked on his father's farm before being given his own plot of land for crops at their wedding. She is accompanied by her mother-in-law, Hallel, a formidable woman with a steely look. I suspect the pressure from Hallel to produce a grandson is not helping this pregnancy happen.

I started seeing her when, after nine moons, there had been no sign of a pregnancy. She receives a weekly womb massage and stimulation using long pieces of fabric to rock her slender frame and bring blood to the area, all helping the womb to wake up to its task. To supplement her food, I've given her a blend of fennel and fenugreek seeds, with the leaf of the red raspberry to have as tea. I instruct her to include many onions, garlic and oats in her diet and to eat mallow leaves at least twice a day. Plus, of course, to pray that God may bless her with a baby.

She had appeared today with the unmistakable look of hope – her blood-time had not come for two moons. Trying not to get too excited, I ask her to lie down on a mat in the shade. "Is it okay if I have a little feel?" I ask, as I oil my hands. I know she is hopeful that I will confirm her desperate wish. "It might be too soon to tell, Denah," I say, trying to keep her expectations low, just in case. But to me she looks and, dare I say it, even smells, pregnant. There is a subtle change to everything about her. She nods and shuts her eyes, afraid to read my face in case it's bad news.

I oil my hands and gently run them over the belly. Very carefully I start from the outside just above her hips and draw into the centre. "Don't startle the womb!" my mother would say. "Introduce yourself with care, then she will tell you all." As a child I thought she meant it would whisper to me and I was both fascinated and horrified. But as I became more experienced, I understood her words better and found she was right. The uterus can tell you so much: where it sits, its size, how it feels. I can feel the energy that comes from it. For some women, the womb vibrates with life. You can feel it as you touch them. For some it's shy and feels as if it is hiding from touch. Those women need more care, more time. When I first massaged Denah, her womb had felt slightly to the side, which may prevent pregnancy. The massage and rocking had helped gently loosen the muscles holding it and allowed it to return to a more natural place.

My hands sweep from outside to in, relaxing and soothing the stomach so I can feel what is happening. It can be too painful for a woman if you have not softened the belly first. Outside to in, and then cupping my hand slightly I sweep very gently into the centre, always in towards the womb. Once I feel those muscles start to relax, I run my hand lower, right to the top of the pelvis, feeling for any change since last I massaged and, there it is. The womb is now centred and, while low down, is bigger, and most definitely harder to the touch. This can only mean one thing: it is growing a life inside.

"Denah," I say, "you are pregnant."

Her eyes start open and her hand flies to her mouth in disbelief. "Really? Truly?" she gasps and starts to cry great hot tears of joy. I'm so pleased for her. I remind her that she must take it easy in this early part, not overexert herself and to ensure she eats well. I make sure I say all of this loudly in front of her mother-in-law.

Hallel's pursed lips soften into a restrained smile as she hears the news, she gives a look of satisfaction and a nod to Denah. "That is good news, good news indeed," she says. It strikes me again what a pressure it is on young wives to produce children, how difficult life can be for women who do not and yet how little control women have over it themselves.

Next up is Ilana, eight moons pregnant with her third child. She is looking well today. She tends to have very hard pregnancies. If she does not take care of herself, she gets pale, weak and listless. After the last birth she lost a great deal of blood and took a long time to recover. For her, I recommended lots of cauliflower, sweet peppers, coriander leaf, lentils and purslane, all foods for making you stronger in pregnancy. It seems she has been following my advice as she is a good colour and seems lively today.

As her two boys play in the sun, watched over by Hadar, we talk about the pregnancy, and what is on her mind. My hands gently massage her belly and then I slip a scarf under her bottom. Any scarf or shawl would do, but mine was my mother's and has lifted, rocked and supported a thousand pregnant women. It is placed horizontally on the floor to Ilana and I get her to lie on the floor with her bottom and hips across this long piece of fabric. I lift the ends and stand above her spreading it out so it supports her hips. Holding the ends and taking her weight, I stand over her and lift her middle slightly. Then I start rocking from side to side, allowing her belly to be taken by the rhythm of the movement. This soft, relaxing motion helps loosen the ligaments, soothe the womb and calm the mother. It is a crucial part of our pregnancy care.

Next, there is a breech baby to be turned for a tired mother of two. Each pregnancy her babies end up upside down and each time, close to the end of the pregnancy, I used the skills passed down in my family to turn them. First, I give her warming chamomile tea to help her relax, then I rock her from side to side, letting the belly sway, moving the hips, the top of the legs and the waist. This rhythmical motion relaxes and soothes the womb and the mother and prepares her for a belly massage, which lulls the womb even more. Finally, when I can feel that the belly has softened and the baby has relaxed into this movement, I very slowly use my hands to bring the baby up out of the pelvis and try to get it to turn from the outside.

"Gently, gently," my mother would say, "slowly, slowly… If it does not go easily, you stop." If you are too vigorous, it may do harm, so the movement is always tempered by what my hands feel. Once this is done, a little more rocking and then slowly, slowly I help the woman roll onto her side and then onto all fours. She must crawl around three times in a small circle. Tomorrow we will check if the baby has turned. If not, we repeat the rocking and the crawling, but only once a week do we try to lift and turn the baby. Today, though, I felt the baby change position slightly, so we will see tomorrow if it has turned itself around.

Gentle massage and manipulation of the baby's position using hands and cloth is such an important tool in my life as a midwife. My great-grandmother had told tales of babies and mothers in the village being lost before women had learnt how to help get them into a better position. Without our expertise, it could be a slow and painful death for both mother and baby. So far, I say a little prayer as I think it, in all these years, I have managed to help so many and lost so few.

From my mother, Levona, I also learnt to listen closely to a baby's heart and health by pressing my head against the mother's belly, checking that the baby sounds strong. I learnt not to be afraid to give bitter herbs to make a woman sick and start labour if the baby regularly sounded sluggish and slow. She showed me how to stop dangerous bleeding after the birth by tucking a sliver of placenta in the mother's cheek. So many ways to help. My mother taught me, and I had taught my daughters in turn. Sometimes our knowledge feels like a gift and a blessing, and sometimes it is a weight of responsibility that wakes me up in the middle of the night. *Have I done the right thing? Is the mother well? Have I done enough?* Benjamin is used to me startling myself awake. He will always wake up enough to check that I am alright then return to a sleep of heavy breathing and a periodic snore.

After that, a mother in her fifth moon with burning wee is needing comfort. I give her a tea made of crushed caraway seeds, hawthorn leaves and peppermint to ease her discomfort. Then the lovely Yaffa comes to see me, still hoping for a son after five daughters. Why she thinks I can help I do not know. I can help a woman get pregnant, but not decide what sex it will be – that is in the hands of God. "We prepare the soil," my grandmother would say, "He gave us the skills to get the ground ready, but it is God who plants the seed of life." Still, it is always a joy to see Yaffa and her children, and I massage her beautiful wrinkled belly, stretched by so many pregnancies and hope that this time she will get her prayer answered.

Through these visits in pregnancy, we get to know the women and bond with them, so that in labour we are a familiar presence, able to read their signals better. They trust us in their most sacred moment because we have advised, comforted and guided them through to this point. We have readied them with nourishing food, massage and adjusting the position of the baby. Though these few hours in my day might look like nothing, they make such a difference to the journey. They mean we travel as a caravan through birth and not alone through the desert.

After I have seen and spoken to all who came today, I go to a post-birth visit to a mother on day twenty of her forty-day confinement. We had seen her throughout her pregnancy, helping relieve symptoms with herbs for sickness, massaged her growing belly to help soothe discomfort and helped with the position of the baby. Today, I go to check her recovery, to see how the baby is doing, and take a small bowl of stew to build her strength.

Every day I make this stew, and every day it is shared among the women in my care. So many women are low in energy after birth, especially if they have lost a lot of blood. I also take fenugreek and caraway seeds with me to make a warming drink and increase her milk production.

I love these visits. We talk, I help guide breastfeeding and, if needed, I will cook a meal for the family. Sometimes I get to sit and hold the baby and just give her a rest. Daily I will massage her belly, checking that her womb feels as if it's returning to shape and helping build her internal strength. This rest and care after birth is so important. A woman's womb is her table of strength, if she is to go on to have more pregnancies and a healthy, long life, it must be cared for in the time after birth.

As I return home, the sun is at its height. I pass through the small market at the centre of our town. Wooden carts and shops with food and pots are laid out for the locals and passing customers. I know all of the stall holders, some for as long as we both can remember.

"How is the family?" "How is business?" I listen to the news (so much news) about family and local happenings as I fill my basket with grains, pulses, herbs and vegetables. At almost every stall the vendors greet me. I have been there as their children or grandchildren were born. I visited their homes and cared for their families. Almost every stall will drop a little extra in my woven basket, "For the mothers," they say.

These gifts will be added to the stew I make for the mothers every day: they are fed by the kindness of a town. A town that remembers how much it helped them when they or their loved ones were in their forty days. No matter if I go to the market every day, the small gifts never fail to make their way to my basket, "For the mothers." These are good people.

As I leave the market, I always pause and look at the mountains that surround us, I love the view but also I'm tired after Talia's birth. Finding shade under one of the many trees, I survey the incredible view, rest and greet those I know who walk by. There are many familiar faces and much to share: tales of who has returned for the census, how children and grandchildren are. But, as in the market, the talk of the day is all about the stars.

My friend Rina, who I have known since my girlhood, stops a while to sit with me. She is on her way to visit her daughter Razili. Rina is short and getting rounder by the year. Her hair is deep black and incredibly curly, falling in beautiful ringlets under her head scarf. Her lined face is creased with years of smiling, deep lines are mapped into her face like the terraces on the hills. They cannot stop her eyes twinkling or her deep laugh carving even more marks across her face. She is a tonic to any tiredness. I was of course her midwife when Rina had her children, and was there when Razili gave birth to her grandchildren. I have been there as the midwife for seven of Rina's grandchildren so far. It's the beauty of being in a town this size, my work is intergenerational.

We hug and sit together in the shade, sharing juicy fresh dates from her basket. We talk about everything, laughing, consoling and counselling each other in turn. Once we've exchanged news, our conversation turns to the building excitement about the imminent astrological event.

Over the last month, two bright stars had been creeping over the night sky, moving closer and closer to each other and with every night inching nearer to being directly overhead. At night the stars above this town are extraordinary anyway, the dark night and clear air makes for a dramatic display of a million twinkling lights, but these two stood out even amid our breath-taking display. All around the town, rumours had spread like wildfire about what it could mean. Oracles had been consulted, and there had been so many more offerings made at the temple to ensure the safety of individuals and families – just in case.

"Apparently at the Roman temples they are saying it means a king will be born," Rina assures me in excited tones. "They have no idea which king though!" She laughs and leans in to whisper conspiratorially, "I hear Herod has no babies due to replace the sons he had killed, the word is that since he killed Mariamne he has become wild with paranoia. He is suspicious of everyone. That poor woman – who would be a wife of Herod, eh?" In these times, this is dangerous talk. Insulting Herod could get you executed, but Rina knows mine are safe ears.

I lower my voice, "Word is that in Jerusalem the Romans have been rounding up street preachers who were deemed to be spreading panic." This is a worry. The Roman invaders in our land keep their power over us with force and words. It is easy to be accused of things you have not said, and it's a tool that has been too often used against any of us who challenge them. I continue, "But I've also heard that the community leaders have met to discuss what this movement in the skies means."

Rina nods thoughtfully, "So it is important...I wonder what it can mean," she says as her eyes gaze out the great expanse of mountains.

"I've heard it heralds disaster," I say earnestly, "and I heard that from Gomer the fruit seller, so it must be true!" We both giggle, the mood again lifted. Gomer loves to be the source of news and the more outlandish the better. You are wise not to put too much store into the words of Gomer.

"Still," I add, "they look like they will join tonight. Whatever will happen, will happen soon."

In truth I do not know what to think. Those of us who work in birth are very mindful of signs. Our instinct is so important to our work and part of that is observing nature. When the moon is full there will be more women who labour or want to see us. They are unsettled or agitated and need reassurance. Indeed, last time there was a night of shooting stars, three women started in labour. Who knows what this star will bring?

"I must go," says Rina, breaking my thoughts. "You look tired Salome. Go home to bed. No doubt another labouring mother will need you soon – who knows, perhaps even when a king is born!" We both howl laughing. Lowly women like us do not attend the births of kings. They have their own family midwives and the finest of treatment. My work is with the ordinary, the hard working, the pretty, the plain, the first timers and those with a houseful of children. We work with those who can afford to pay us and those who cannot. It mostly balances out.

We hug goodbye and Rina heads off waving joyfully as she goes. I sit for another few minutes enjoying the view before I head home.

Bethlehem sits on the top of a hill, surrounded by mountains of sandy earth, in terraces and slopes. The entire landscape is dotted with olive and almond trees as far as the eye can see. Sheep are visible on the hills and around the town, watched over by shepherds who follow them across this rugged landscape. Every year wheat grows on the slopes up the hill towards the peak, the golden heads wave in the hazy heat, rippling in the breeze that brings hot air over the mountains. It's so abundant here that the name Bethlehem translates as "The House of Bread". I love that this town, home to the House of David, feeds and provides for us with such riches.

When the wheat is harvested, the shepherds bring the sheep to the outskirts of town to eat the remaining grains and stubble, and they in turn fertilise the ground for next year. These are no ordinary sheep, however, as close by here is Migdal Eder – The Tower of the Flock. The Migdal is a circular stone tower, just two storeys high but with a viewing platform on the second level, allowing the shepherds to watch over their flocks whatever the weather.

As with all the buildings in Bethlehem it is made with the rocks of the area and mud from the ground. Everything here fits into the landscape. Our buildings blend in with the land around, as does the tower, with only its wooden roof separating it from the mountains. On the ground floor is a safe, warm place to keep sheep during labour, where the shepherds take their rest and can care for newborn lambs. This shepherding role is even more important here as here on these hills are bred the sacrificial lambs that will be used in the Jerusalem temples. A firstborn male lamb born in the shadow of Migdal Eder is considered holy and is to be used for sacrifice. To be used it must not only be born in the shadow but also live outside for a full year and be completely without injury or blemish.

The shepherds who look after them are not like ordinary shepherds, wild and untamed. These shepherds are Levites, associated with the Temple of Jerusalem – they are religious men in their own right. They decide which are to be the Passover lambs. You can tell them by the cloaks they wear, made of good quality dark grey wool. They are well respected in Bethlehem, as it is a great honour for our small town to supply so many of the holiest lambs. So precious are these lambs, and so unblemished must they remain, that some are even swaddled by the shepherds. This keeps them completely free from stain, so that they are pure enough to be used in the holiest of our temples.

We have much in common, the shepherds and we midwives. We watch our flocks, we observe the signs that the birth is coming, we help only when necessary and will work all night to save a mother or baby if needed. We are allowed to pass with our work in places not everyone can go. We can work at times that others cannot. We are out in all weather, and care for every single one of our flock. We are servants to the cycle of life.

The sheep fertilise the ground, and provide us with so many wild and free foods. Children are taught foraging as play from a young age. They are sent with older children to the fields around us and gather the edible plants, mindful to always leave enough for the plants to survive ("take no more than half," the grandmothers shout). They bring back handfuls of purslane, oregano, dandelions and berries that grow so readily on these hills. This land provides us with so many wild plants and herbs. Here we dine on fruits, leaves, beans, grains, beautiful breads, our own olives and nuts, and occasionally the meat of the sheep. We are very blessed.

You would not think that up here, on a hill surrounded by hot dry mountains, we would be so blessed with such abundant food. You would think that water would be scarce, making it impossible for so many of us to carve a life out on these desert rocks. But underneath her, Bethlehem holds a secret. She sits on a great underground lake, an aquifer that provides a water source big enough not only for us, but also Jerusalem. In truth it is why we are here, a town to guard the precious water supply below. Earth, water, heat and an abundance of plants to feed us. No wonder we feel blessed, with so many of God's gifts surrounding us.

Earth, water, desert winds and now a sign in the sky. Something makes me involuntarily shiver. It's that feeling you get sometimes when your whole body reacts to an unseen cold breath. I realise I do think the stars mean something. A change perhaps? Something starting? An arrival? I don't know what, but something…

I gather my basket and head home uplifted by my time with Rina. By the time I get home I am exhausted and take, as most do, a small sleep in this, the hottest part of the day, when the air is so stifling that there is nothing to be done but retreat to the coolness of the house and rest. Benjamin is working in his shaded workshop. I can hear the rhythm of his taps as he gently shapes and creates beautiful woodwork. It has been the music to our years of marriage and is the most comforting sound to my ears.

I can tell by the way he taps the wood that he is happy. You can always tell by the rhythm of his work. He is a calm, peaceful man but when he needs to release his anger, perhaps annoyed by a merchant or a difficult client, he will work faster and harder. Then I may hear hammering or sawing. Today though, the sound of chiselling is playful and light, like water bouncing over stones. He and the wood are bound together. He understands its curves, its knots, its bend and flex, knowing how far it can be shaped and when to stop; he tests gently but with a firm hand. When first getting a piece of wood he will examine it, get to know it, touch it, before he starts to work, just as he did with the girls when they were babies. He watched them first, smiling in delight as they unfurled in front of us. He waited to understand the shape of their wood, where their knots were and how best to work with them. He has been, for the whole of their lives, a loving, kind presence, always proud of these masterpieces we created.

The steady tapping lulls my eyes closed and I fall asleep, dreaming of stars.

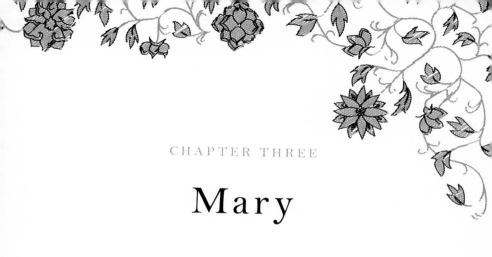

CHAPTER THREE

Mary

The knock came to our door early in the evening as the sun was setting. It was scarcely heard over the sound of chatter in the house. My husband's younger brother along with his wife and five children have not long arrived, bringing gifts, noise, stories and the delight of a reunion after many months apart. We are missing Shifra, the orchestrator of games and distractions for the little ones, as she is at the house of a neighbour who had given birth two weeks ago. She is helping with the smaller children while the mother observes the forty days of rest after birth.

At the door is a round-faced servant girl, Rachel, from the house of my friend Leah, sent to ask for my help. Leah and I had met through our husbands some fifteen years ago – they had attended temple together as boys and had themselves over thirty years of friendship. In the early years, I would regularly see her at celebrations and events. We had found each other easy, agreeable company and before long had become friends in our own right.

The servant girl shared that someone was in labour and they expected the baby to be born that night, her voice heavy with concern. I was puzzled. Leah and her husband, Gad, a leatherworker of some skill, had never been blessed with children. It had been such a source of heartache over the years, so I'm sure she would have told me if a member of her household was expecting. With so many people moving at this time, it must be someone from out of town.

"I'll go," I say to Martha, "I feel I should be there for Leah. Can you please stay and take care of everyone? Make sure that stew gets stirred, and don't forget to add the rosemary. Hadar knows what needs doing." Martha nods. I know they will be fine, their aunties will help and we have most of the food preparation done already.

Once again, I find myself readying to attend the labour of a stranger. Almost always I know the mothers before I help with their births, yet this would be the second birth in as many days where I was with women who were unknown to me. Ordinarily no woman would be travelling and visiting away from home so close to her delivery time. But this was no ordinary time. The census was bringing families back together for a brief period – so many people on the move.

I went around the house gathering my readied supplies, food and birthstones. In a house you might have a birth stool, but as our ancestors were always moving they would carry smaller birthstones instead. From our days of exile in the desert, women found a way to keep the tradition. The birthstones are heavy to carry but we would feel lost without them.

Already cleaned and wrapped, the birthstones comprise of two flat stones that the women in our family, and women that we have cared for, have stood on through the generations to birth. After so much use mine are now smooth, with foot-shaped imprints where birthing feet have gradually worn away the soft stone, leaving smooth spaces for each new labouring mother. These dips are a reminder of this rite of passage that is birth, connecting her with all of the women who have also stood on these stones and roared their baby out. These stones have birthed untold numbers of the babies of the tribes of Bethlehem.

It is the job of the midwife to keep the stones: the holder of the stones is the birthkeeper. She who holds the wisdom of birth.

Birth runs in the blood of the women of this family. Skills passed down from generation to generation of serving women at this most sacred time. All the tools of my trade were handed down to me from my mother, and to her from her mother, and our grandmothers before that. Birth was our trade, our skill, our lives' work. My mother's hands helped so many babies into this world. She was a master of her art, able to soothe the most distressed woman, but also to manipulate, move and help those babies who would otherwise have been lost. I have seen her turn a baby thought past help, bring back from the brink of death a mother worn out and bleeding beyond measure. She knew the herbs, the words to comfort and encourage, the prayers. She taught me and I in turn have taught my daughters.

From the olive wood cabinet that Benjamin had built for my supplies, I pack fresh swaddling blankets, herbs for helping with the pain, herbs for bleeding, some for purifying. I pack the flower of birth, a dried Jericho rose, which grows in these parts. The rose has been used in childbirth since our people can remember. A white flowering shrub, it grows close to the ground with small grey leaves, although this stage does not last long before it withers in the heat to a ball of gnarly twigs with tiny bulbous seed pods. In this dried-out state it waits in the sandy soil for rain, looking to all as though it has died, until, activated by water, it opens again and releases its seeds. During labour, the rose is put into hot water and gradually opens as the woman opens for birth. How easily it opens will predict how easily this baby will be born. Sipping the infused water can help move the birth along, and the infusion is drunk to help women birth, strengthen their womb, and help prevent haemorrhaging.

All these supplies are wrapped up and placed in my basket along with some food. Most often we are fed, but you never know. If we have some made, we take comforting and nourishing breads packed with fruit for the mother. Sweet fruits melted in the dough, kneaded with love and thought of the birth ahead: dates to give energy and comfort, herbs, each for their role in birth, gathered at the most potent moon time.

I say goodbye to everyone and lastly to Benjamin, who kisses my head before sending me on my way. "Take care. Blessings, my love, on you and this woman." He is such a good husband, supporting me to continue this important work and not insisting I just care for him.

I leave with the servant girl, Rachel, into the hot dusty evening. The sun is low, the earth reddened by the light. We walk together through the busy streets. So many people moving. Every so often a face greets me, hands outstretched. Once you have helped a woman deliver her baby, she will never forget you. If it went well, you are always blessed in her eyes. If it did not…

We never forget, you know, not one of those lost ones. No, the babies and the mothers we have lost, they are, each one, played over and over in our heads, every detail, every moment, looking for a way to make it right. Pull the cloak tighter. *You did your best* you tell yourself and, as God is my witness, I always did. Sometimes the baby would be dead already, or the mother past saving but…see, again here I am looking for a way to make it better and yet…

In my head that 'if only' sometimes circles like a dog readying to sleep. *If the baby had only…if only I had been able to…if I had only been there sooner…or able to stop the bleeding.* Life and death are so very close in our work. So many mothers are lost in this act of creation. We are there at the start of life, but I have seen Death stalking with my own eyes, felt its presence in the room, watched the life slip away from a mother during or after birth. As midwives, we are the handmaidens of life itself. We help bring these new fledgling lives into the world, and yet so often are also there as it is snatched away. It's a heavy price for growing and bringing forth a child. This is the risk the mother must face as she births her baby, and we are her guardians. This is our risk too. We, as the guardians, would sometimes pay the price for a baby lost. Too many times midwives have been blamed for the loss of a baby, even killed. Powerful families can extract revenge without fear of repercussion.

On we walk, the sun setting low and fast, past the Roman centurions standing at the gateways, swords at the hilt, helmets disguising their faces just enough to make them all look indistinguishable. A vast army in our land. They kept the peace, but oh the brutality of these people. It is because of them our town is so full: at the command of the Emperor, everyone must return to their hometown to declare that they exist, no doubt so that we can pay yet more taxes.

We are heading to the centre of the town. These were among the first houses here in Bethlehem, nestled into a bank of stone, starting as caves or overhangs with houses gradually being built around.

Leah's house is big, but not well-kept like the home of Miriam and Adam. The front door is old and has expanded and contracted so many times it no longer looks as if it fits properly. The rocks around the door have crumbled slightly, but as we touch the *mezuzah* and enter, it is clear that it is cared for and tidy inside. A tiny woman, with a huge chest and wiry grey hair, bustles towards us, her face lined with the patterns of a life of hard work, much concentrating and much squinting from the sun. Some people's lines come from smiling, others are formed by years of disapproving. But there is no malice in Leah's face, she is hard-working, level and kind.

"Thank you for coming, Salome. Thank you. Welcome. Are you all well?" she asks, but does not pause long enough for a reply. Her hands are beckoning us back out of the front door. She speaks with urgency and fluster. "I have so much to do. We have a house full of guests. So many members of the family are here for the census and I must feed everyone…but this girl arrived and she is…" she breaks off to give an instruction about checking the food to a servant girl and without pausing for breath launches back in again "…so pregnant and looking as if she is in labour."

She continues in a long breath, "I was shocked when they arrived at the door. The husband, his name is Joseph, is the son of my cousin. I was not expecting the baby to arrive this soon. They were supposed to return to Nazareth before the baby was born. They came with a note from my cousin asking for my help and explaining their…" she hesitates for a split second, "…*situation*." The word is slow and deliberate. She lowers her voice, "Gad said we should not have them if they might bring shame on us, but I told him they were staying. *Honour,* he kept muttering about honour." I'm a little confused and really not sure what she means, was this baby conceived out of wedlock? That would be a huge source of shame for a family… but it is not clear what is going on.

She doesn't pause for breath, words just flow out, "I'd help her myself, but I must go and attend to our guests. We have nowhere for them in the house, every room is taken. But I am just thankful she made it to us. She might have given birth on the road! On the road, I tell you!" She steps past me, leading back outside the house and starts walking across the front to the side of the building. I am puzzled but follow. Why are we not going in the house?

"Quickly, quickly!" she says, leading me to a door.

"We can't have her in the house as she is in *yoledet*." Once women have had a show, their waters break, or contraction pain becomes regular, they are in a state of *yoledet* and must be separate from the men. This is when our women retreat to the red tent or women's room, just as we do when we are in blood-time. It's the same during and after birth, it is our custom, it is our way.

She continues and turns to look at me directly to make sure I don't object to her decision, "…so she's in the stable."

I manage to stop the shock in my face and nod with understanding. I am shocked though – *the stable?* She is not an animal! But I think I understand Leah's dilemma. If this house has no room for women in their blood-time, this must be the only place Leah had available. I suppose I should be glad this poor couple were not left to have their baby on the road.

We have reached the door of a simple stable, half in a cave under the rock overhang and then extended with rocks and stones, using the outside wall of the house as one side. Stables in a house are usually part of the inner courtyard, but this one may have been there before the house was built, and the house built up around it.

We knock and open the door. Leah steps in before me and I follow, clutching my bags. The space is much more pleasant than I was expecting, but still unmistakably a stable. From the dust of the road we step onto hardened earth, made compact and solid by years of use, sloped to a channel through the middle and out the side, allowing water and waste to run away. It is thankfully dry. The room is a good size, they could keep a number of animals in here if needed. The walls are rough but solid, the same sandy stone stuck together with mortar but, as this is just a space for animals, the inside had not been coated with plaster, leaving the rough rocks on show.

The room is divided by roof-supporting pillars, creating stalls made of half height dividing walls. The room is lit by a small oil lamp on an upturned box on the floor. Above us, the beams can be seen, on top of which sit the dark pattern of branches and clay that make up the roof. An animal smell hangs in the air, but does not overpower, even though there is a heavily pregnant ewe in one corner and a dusty looking brown donkey in another tied to a post and munching a big pile of hay. That must have been the donkey they arrived on. At the very back of the space I can see the outline of tall grain and wine pots, lining almost an entire wall. The cave-like environment made a perfect temperature for storage.

"I've brought you the midwife," said Leah, her voice softening as we come into view of a couple standing by the last low wall, using it as a protection between the entrance and themselves at the back of the space. Partly hidden from view as you first walk in, the stall divider offered them a small degree of privacy. The labouring woman was using the wall as support during her contraction and had not seen us enter. She was drifting in and out of the focus required to work through the sensation of a contraction peak.

The woman looks only slightly older than my Martha. As first-time mothers tend to be, this girl is slim apart from her bump. She is wearing a tunic of pale blue, a good quality fabric with delicate embroidery around the edges in a red thread, the red colour matching the protective red thread bracelet around her wrist. Her clothes and skin look dusty and her bare feet have sandal marks carved out in desert sand. Her smooth black hair is coming out of the cloth she had used to tie it, long strands are falling down across her face and sticking to the sweat on her cheeks.

Her skin is golden but still dusty from the desert. She has the beautiful dark eyebrows and eyelashes that make the women of this region so striking, with strong cheekbones and a straight nose. She is not beautiful in the same way Talia had been, but her face is kind, with a mouth that smiles even when not trying. I watch as she entirely focuses on blowing the sensations out of her body as she leans forwards, rocks and breathes.

Next to her is a tall man with the traditional long hair and beard of the men of these parts. He is in a dusty, earth-coloured tunic with a traditional fringed over-cloak. His oval face is gentle and full of concern. His beard makes him look a little older, but I suspect he has not been a man for many years. I'm finding it hard not to be angry with him. *Why would you bring a labouring woman this far from home? Why would you not leave her with family?* She does not need to be with him for the census. We women are treated as belongings by the Romans, not individuals who have to present themselves. *What kind of a man would make a heavily pregnant woman travel this close to her time?* I hope my face does not betray my thoughts. This woman must feel safe with me. It is her I am here for.

Hearing Leah speak, the mother looks up and nods at us with grateful eyes and says, "Thank you, aunty." She then leans back again, shutting her eyes, rocking, and breathing heavily through the sensation. I wait, saying no more. It is not good to disturb a woman during a contraction. We will speak when this one is done. She sways in a movement like a dance so common in women giving birth. No matter where they are from, whether it is their first or twelfth baby, this dance of grounded feet and swaying hips is universal to women in labour. It is a dance our bodies know without our heads having to teach it. A dance as old as birth itself.

As the contraction fades, the woman straightens up. With her eyes still closed, she lets go of the pillar and moves a hand to rub her full belly. Then she opens her eyes. This is my cue and I step forward. It's only a few steps past the donkey and into the small, nest-like space they have made behind the divider. Fresh hay is laid out on the ground. Their bed rolls are placed neatly in a corner along with their travel packs. There is a jug of water and stone cups on a small table that has been brought in from the house. Next to the jug there is a platter of fruit: pomegranate, grapes and oranges, along with two bread rolls, and a small jug of olive oil. Someone has emptied the stone feeding trough and lined it with hay and sheepskin. On the floor there is a small woven basket ready to hold the placenta.

I speak, introducing myself first. "I am Salome, I'm a midwife and am here to help you." It's a funny thing but those are the words my mother always used. She never said, "I'm here to deliver your baby." She always said, "I'm here to help you." It had taken me years to notice, but it spoke volumes about her. She was always about the woman, never about her role in the birth. She first and foremost served women in birth. It was her act of devotion, her holiest role.

The man speaks first, his voice is soft and measured. "This is my wife, Mary, I am Joseph. Thank you. Thank you for coming to us. I don't think she has long to go."

I can't help myself and respond far too quickly and firmly, "You should not have been on the road with her in this condition." The words are out. I see the woman flinch. This is not making her feel at ease. I must regain her trust or this birth may be affected. Bad feeling or mistrust in a birth room can slow or stall a labour. I've felt a cervix close back together when a woman is disturbed or treated badly. I am here for her and this baby, and so I quickly follow with, "Well, we are all here now and you have found somewhere safe and cosy to be. How lovely that you have made a bed for this baby already." I smile at the trough already prepared as a bed. The distraction works and they smile in unison.

"It is not much, but it will do," says Mary. Her voice is low and melodic.

Joseph takes a breath, "You are right, I am sorry, but it was not..." He hesitates as if to find the right words. "It was not the right thing to leave Mary with my family." Ah, perhaps I have been too hasty. Here is a man who on first meeting me has been respectful enough to apologise to me, even though I spoke harshly. This is something many men would not do even if they were wrong: they see women as lesser objects. Clearly there is more to this story than meets the eye. Now I want to know why he could not leave her at their home. Before I can ask anything further, another contraction begins.

Leah looks at Joseph expectantly. Now Mary is in established labour, we are really in the world of women, he should not be here anymore. In an emergency men will attend when there is absolutely no one else, but really this is women's work and he should be outside saying the prayers to bless this baby on its journey from inside to out, from God's care to earthly care, in the hands of women.

The contraction is starting to rise in intensity. I put down my bags and, pouring a small amount of water on my hands from the jug, wash them over the drain that runs out through the front of the building. I mutter a prayer as my hands perform the familiar task. *"My help is from the Lord, the Maker of heaven and earth,"* while I watch to see how far along this labour is.

Mary moans, leans forwards, once again holding onto the pillar, swaying her hips slowly, breathing out in a long moaning sound. Her head flops forwards and even more hair comes free, covering her face. She is still dressed so I cannot see her bump and how it is responding to a contraction, nor check to see if the birthline is appearing on her bottom. I want to feel her legs, as their temperature can indicate progress, but cannot do that until this contraction is ended. I will have to judge progress based on her behaviour, the intensity of contractions and a lifetime of experience of watching birth unfold.

The contractions look powerful, they are requiring all Mary's focus. With strong breaths, each one takes a slow minute to pass. I think this baby will be here soon.

"It may not be long now, Joseph. I can look after her now." He hesitates, as if unsure what to do. I feel for him. It must be so hard to leave her with a stranger. Here, as well, if Leah cannot stay, there will be no family present, no one the mother knows and trusts. I have only just met them and he has to leave her with me. No wonder he pauses.

He does something I am not expecting: he leans forward and asks Mary if she would like him to stay. I have never seen a man ask this before. She straightens up and turns to face him. I try not to listen. "I am safe with this woman. You go and pray. Stay close. God will be with me. I love you."

My heart melts a little. I see so many relationships in this work. Men who do not care. Men who only care about having a son. Men who care nothing for the baby or the mother. Some who love their women so much that seeing or hearing them go through the pain of labour is torture. Some who do not even say the protective prayers, and some who care only for the spectacle of praying. My favourites are couples like this. The couples who really, deeply care for each other. It reminds me of how Benjamin and I were, and still are.

He very gently whispers something to her, then moves with Leah towards the door. He is still slightly reluctant to leave, Mary smiles reassuringly but not entirely convincingly at him. I think she is saying it as much for herself as him when she says, "Go, I am safe now." She takes my hand.

This gives him the confidence he needs and he steps out, stooping slightly to get through the door with Leah following him more reluctantly than I'd expected. I think she would like to stay herself and see this baby born. She hovers at the threshold. "I'm so sorry," she says to Mary, "I have so much to do, but Salome has been my friend since I met your uncle and will take such good care of you."

She turns to me and with a grateful smile says, "Send Joseph if you need anything, anything at all – and thank you, Salome," before following Joseph out and returning to her busy house. Joseph is now stationed outside the door. No one can disturb us. He guards us with his prayers and presence.

It's a funny thing that happens when the men leave the room at a birth. The atmosphere relaxes. We are in a space we know from when we have our first blood-time: the space of women. No need for modesty or masking sounds. We are women together, most of whom have seen a birth, have given birth. We have felt the power, the sweat, the stretching and the soul-wrenching opening and letting go that it takes to bring forth life. We can let go in the company of our sisters.

Mary's face changes. She has been, as many women do, silently carrying the load of the pain. I suspect she did not want to let Joseph know how difficult the journey was. As soon as he is gone, the weight she has carried becomes apparent. Her smile drops and her shoulders pull up to her ears.

"This is so hard," she whispers to me. Her eyes fill up with tears, "I am so grateful to be here. I was afraid I might give birth by the roadside."

I hug her. This complete stranger is like a child in my arms. "Oh, you poor thing," I say. "You have been so brave. You are safe now."

I feel so protective of her, alone in a stable in a strange town, miles from her home and support. I can't help thinking about Joseph's comment that she wasn't safe to leave, and Leah's remark about their 'situation'. Either she was not the choice of the family or – wait a minute, what had Leah said? – that the baby was not due yet, that she expected them to return to Nazareth? I can't help thinking this baby must have been conceived out of wedlock. That might explain why Gad was so reluctant to have them in the house, and why Joseph did not leave her with family. And that journey, the poor thing had come such a long way walking and on a donkey. Not the most comfortable creatures to ride on at the best of times. I could only imagine how sore she must have felt having been jigged up and down for so many miles over such rough terrain.

In truth, while I have reassured her, I don't know that she is safe. If she has been on the donkey a long time, it may have harmed the baby. "How long were you travelling?" I ask, trying to keep my concern from my voice.

"We came from Nazareth, we travelled south along the flatlands and then through the mountains. It is a journey I have taken every year to go to Jerusalem with my family but…" she patted her bump, "this was the hardest it has ever been. I do not know what I would have done without our donkey!" She looks over to the corner where the small creature is chewing hay.

"The last few miles were so, so hard," she says, a grimace across her face giving away how hard it has been for her. "I could feel the pains starting… We could not find this house. We knocked on every door."

Mary has softened into my hug. She is a woman used to being loved, that is a good sign and important to know. Women who have had a lifetime of harsh treatment respond differently to physical care or touch. They cannot trust that the care is not a trick or they simply have never experienced it. My heart breaks for those who have never been loved. The damage done to people can take so long to heal and sometimes cannot ever do so. I do not feel this from Mary, she has already shown a confidence that comes from a life of kindness. This is good.

I ask her if she has lost any water. She shakes her head. She had been losing a bloody discharge in the last hours but no liquid. It's too soon after meeting her and Joseph leaving to ask her if she has felt the baby move recently. I don't want to worry her, but I am always conscious that in my work Death is rarely far away.

Sometimes Death comes for the mother, sometimes for the baby. Sometimes both. As a midwife I feel like the line of defence, with me between the woman and Death, stalking the birth room drawn in by the crossing of a soul from the otherworld to ours. I pray in my head, always, for the mother and the baby.

The Lord is your Guardian; the Lord is your shadow; by your right hand. By day, the sun will not smite you, nor will the moon at night. The Lord will guard you from all evil; He will guard your soul. The Lord will guard your going out and your coming in from now and to eternity.

Another contraction is starting, perhaps because she had relaxed in the hug, perhaps because she was no longer trying to hide the intensity to protect Joseph, but it catches her unawares and she lets out a cry of pain as it builds. I hold her tight in my arms and reassure her, "You are safe. Breathe it out Mary, breathe it out." The use of breathing is the key to staying on top of the sensations. When women hold their breath, it is as if they hold the pain. Their body remains tense and everything hurts. They need to breathe.

"Release, release," my mother would whisper to women. "Your body knows what to do… Breathe. Let go."

Mary looks up at me, eyes wide with pain and a hint of fear as she tries to get her breath back. "Ow, ow, ow!" comes out. "Owwwwwwww!" it is still building. She grips me tightly and locking eyes copies my long breath out.

"Breathe. Let it go," I whisper. Her shoulders drop as she pushes a long breath out just as she reaches the peak and then over the top of the sensation as it begins to fade. It takes just a short while longer to disappear completely. As the final tightness leaves her body, Mary sinks into me again. I give her a moment but I need to be ready before the next contraction begins.

"Are you happy here? Shall I place the birthstones underneath you?" I ask. Mary's face breaks into a warm smile, the creases around her forehead relaxing.

"You brought some? I did not think I would have any. Thank you," and then she adds, "I hope they were not too heavy."

I release her and unwrap the two thin pale sandstone rectangles. They are flat on one side with a slightly sandy feel, but the other side is worn by generations of feet. They are thin enough to carry without being impossibly heavy, but thick enough to take the weight of a labouring woman. Mary places her feet on each stone as I place them under her. Each one has been in my family for generations. Each one has been with me or my mother and grandmothers before me to many, many births. Our ancestors took stones with them across the desert and now I carry these in my kit.

Perhaps it is just a trick of the mind that gives strength from standing on the stones that so many before have given birth on. Perhaps it is the feel of this smoothed cool stone underfoot that works such magic on a woman in labour. Perhaps there really are traces of the strength of every woman who has laboured before her on the stones left in them, rising up through the legs to the woman's womb and heart. Who knows how God chooses to work? Perhaps the stones are a gift from God to women – the tablets containing knowledge about how to birth.

The next contraction is already beginning. Mary gives me a nod to signal it is starting. As I am there, I ask her if I can feel her legs. They are cold, right up to her knees.

This contraction is strong. Mary's breathing starts to get very deep and a low long sound starts to come out with her breath. She is now standing on the stones and I move to be between her and the closed stable door. She's dropping lower and lower, bending her knees and leaning to let her belly hang. It is amazing to watch her instinctual behaviour kick in: moan, rock, lean. Our bodies know how to birth like we know how to breathe. I hold my hands on her. I lean in and move as she moves. It is a shared rhythm.

"You are doing so well," I whisper to her, "…so well." In the quiet of the stable, with the sound of the donkey chewing and the ewe scrabbling in the hay, we stand as a joined three: mother, midwife and the baby we have not yet met. All gently swaying until the contraction is finished.

At the end of the contraction I reach back to my basket and find a small wrapped piece of honeycomb and a wrap containing a rose of Jericho, the flower of birth. I've just about got them to the small table when another contraction begins. Mary leans forward and I rush to her side and again put my hand on her and rub her back as she leans and rocks, leans and rocks.

It is another strong one. Occasionally Mary will cry out as the pain hits. The sweat is pouring off her and me in this quiet space. When this is done, I offer her a sip of water from the goblet. She drinks thirstily, her mouth dry from the long out-breaths. I then drop the rose into the jug so that it can open and infuse the water.

I break off a tiny corner of the honeycomb and give it to her to eat. It will give her strength for the pushing that I suspect is not far off. Soon she leans forward again. I start to rub her back. There is so little time between each one. As it's just about to build I ask her if I can feel her bump during the pain. Mary does not open her eyes but nods. As the contraction builds, I put a hand on her bump. Even through her tunic I can feel the strength of the tightness. The bump bulges forward and changes shape in my hand. We breathe and rock, breathe and rock as I feel the power of her womb pushing forward and down to bring this baby out.

The contractions are getting so close now, there is barely time to reset ourselves before the next one rises. Mary is working so hard, huge breaths as her womb works to bring this baby down. Standing on the stones, she uses the well-worn wood of the pillar to hold on to. It is smoothed by years of use and thankfully will not harm her hands as she uses it to hold her weight. She looks so hot and is dripping with sweat. She is still in her tunic but I understand why she has not undressed. This is just a stable. Anyone could walk in and she is with a stranger. This is so unlike most births I attend where women are somewhere they know and feel safe and they will almost always have met me multiple times in their pregnancy or previous births. I worry though that she will get too hot. Even as the sun sets, the heat does not leave this town immediately. Or, if her clothes are soaked or stained, does she even have more? I decide that if she doesn't I will go and get some from my home. She is almost the same size as my Martha.

The waiting of birth always feels like a sacred time, as if everything else stands still while this incredible process takes place. It is always a surprise when you remember it has not. Every so often a noise from the road outside, a shout or greeting, the neigh of the donkey or the bleat of the ewe in the corner reminds us that there is a world outside of this moment. Life is going on in full force outside this little stable in Bethlehem, as evening falls. Families eating, prayers being said, friends laughing, livestock being herded to shelter for the night. All but a few are completely oblivious to us, as we are cocooned in our little space, working to bring this baby into the world.

I had been right: it was not to be long. Suddenly, Mary's demeanour changes. Whereas before she had found her rhythm to get her through each contraction – it would start, she would signal me it was beginning and I would rub the very top of her hips and across her bottom, she would lean forward sway and blow out the sensations in huge great breaths – but now, very abruptly, she looks up at me with wide, slightly scared eyes.

"I need to puussshhhh," she says, pushing with the word. Her face changes as she uses her breath and the words to push down, as if expelling the air from her down through to her legs. This is the part where you get a thrill of both excitement and fear as a midwife. This is the beginning of the end of this birth.

Many women struggle at this point. Women who have been coping beautifully can suddenly become overwhelmed: sometimes they shake like a leaf in the wind, sometimes they lose all sense of themselves and start to fear that they cannot do it. I think of it as the last mountain before you reach the Promised Land. It's the way out of the desert, but it comes at the point where you feel so weak and the mountain looks so high. At this moment in a birth, I often think of our ancestors: Moses, Miriam and Aaron leading my people, the Israelites, away from slavery through the desert for forty years. That final stretch, knowing the end is close at hand but having to find the strength to keep going, having to trust that the Promised Land will be over this last hurdle. Trusting in the Lord to keep going. It is so easy to lose faith, to doubt. Even Moses benefited from the support of Aaron and Miriam to help and guide him through the years. Similarly, women in labour have the support of their midwife, the voice of faith and encouragement at this, the last stretch of the journey. We stand with and by them, physically and spiritually, when they have these moments of fear or doubt.

"Pushing is good! It's nearly time to meet your baby. Just do whatever your body wants to do," I whisper. She nods, sweat glistening across her face. And then, with a long low sigh, almost a whimper, a small tear trickles down her face. A sudden seriousness has entered the room.

"What if I can't do it? What if something is wrong?" she whispers, her eyes scared.

This fear is very common as women reach the birth of their baby. I have seen it a thousand times, as women cross the threshold into the space where their baby leaves them, they show what I can only describe as grief. It can look like fear, upset, loss of control. Sometimes they will shake or cry. Sometimes they will say things they do not mean or think. It does not last, like grief, but it is overwhelming while they feel it. My mother always told me to watch for this sudden change. "The baby will follow soon after," she would say and over the years, I saw she was right.

I lean in and stroke the hair from Mary's face as if she were one of my own daughters. "You can do it. You are doing it. This baby is coming," I reassure her. She looks at me with grateful eyes, until the pain distracts her and she again moans and breathes and pushes down. I hitch up her tunic and tie it in a knot at her hip height, revealing slim but strong brown legs, still dusty from the journey. This contraction lasts a long time. As it ends, I reach for some clean hay and lay it underneath her. It will not be long.

After the next contraction, I go to my basket, find a clean piece of cloth with which to wrap the baby and hang it over the makeshift crib. When the contraction begins, Mary again lowers herself, knees bending to take her closer to the ground and the birthstones, with a huge roar and push. I crouch down by her. When a mother is birthing upright, be it on a birth stool, standing, kneeling or squatting close to the ground, I must be lower to see what is happening. This gets less and less easy as my bones get older. I squat on my heels so that I can be ready to watch as she pushes. Every so often a baby will come unexpectedly fast and when the mother is standing you must be ready.

As the contraction ends, she does not straighten up fully but leans on the wood letting her belly hang.

The next contraction comes, and, as Mary moans, I see her opening. A slight bulge is starting to appear. As she roars and pushes, the bulge appears until the contraction ends, then it retracts back inside her. As the waters haven't yet broken I know this is the sac of waters but the baby is close behind that bulge.

I offer her a sip to drink, all the time encouraging and soothing her as she is shaky, tired and starting to lose her calm. Fear can creep up on women during birth, looking for those who are not well-supported and cared for and those who do not have reassuring hands to calm them down. It can slow or even stop the labour and potentially harm the baby by keeping them in too long. I wish I had Martha or Shifra with me. Mary really would have benefited from having two of us to support and care for her. I need to keep the fear at bay, it is rising like a mist on the mountains.

It is hard to know, having only just met her, what will work. For some women it is physical contact, massage and warming oils. Many women just want their own mothers to comfort them like a small child. For some it is talking about the end of the pain. For others it is thinking about meeting their baby. Some focus on the contraction, others on a point, a breath or a prayer. Often, listening to the men praying outside the room helps, the comforting repetition of a familiar psalm is a soothing sound to latch onto. But we cannot hear Joseph. He is out there alone, listening to his wife's cries and praying quietly in the dark Bethlehem night. We are cocooned in this little stall, while he keeps vigil for us outside.

I am already low down, so I start by placing my hands over her feet, which in turn are on the birthstones. Sitting on the hardened earth, this grounding is a good place to start. "Mary," I say gently. "I can see your baby coming. You are nearly there." This news, just as it had with Talia, reanimates Mary. Too often women do not believe that they are progressing and that the work they do to bring their babies down is working.

"Have faith," I say. "God is with you." To us, birth, whatever the outcome, is a gift from God, and the spiritual side is of huge importance in our culture. My words have an unexpected effect. Mary locks eyes with me as if something very important that had been lost in the waves of the sensations has just resurfaced.

She quietly repeats my words, "God is with me. God is with me. God is with me." I feel a shift in her and around her, a small smile forms at the corner of her mouth. "Thank you, Salome, how could I have forgotten that? God is with me."

She takes a big breath and this time as the contraction starts she has a much calmer expression. She pushes, hands clenched to white on the wood. I see the bulge again, much further forward this time. She pauses to breathe and then pushes again taking guidance from the sensations in her body.

The waters are bulging ahead of the baby. In the dim light, they look whitish, which is good as it means the baby is not distressed. Some midwives will break the waters as the baby emerges but my mother taught me to leave it alone, as babies born in the sac are calmer, protected as they leave the womb and enter our world. They say to be born with the sac intact is auspicious. They say that it's a sign a baby will be a great leader and it might be, we midwives are very mindful of signs, but I think it is also a sign of a gentle midwife.

Mary's thighs are glistening with sweat and trembling as she rests between contractions. I give her legs a vigorous rub which helps release the tension she's holding there. Soon, another contraction is rising, and Mary is letting out a long breath and pushing down, baby bulging as she opens. Her breath ends with a shudder and the baby sits there, no longer retreating back as it was before. We have a few minutes before the next one begins.

"Mary," I say. "Soon I will ask that you take short breaths. It will stop you pushing so that the baby does not come too fast." She raises her head enough to nod. Another contraction soon begins and this time she cries out as the baby's head stretches her wide. "Pant now!" I urge. I squat down in front of her ready to catch this baby. Peering up as I hear Mary panting, I watch the incredible stretch as the waters and the baby's head emerges.

"You're doing it, baby is coming! Keep panting!" Mary does as I say. Pain is etched across her face and then the contraction finishes. The sweat drips down from her head and onto her blue tunic darkening it where it lands. The baby's head is there, still held in a milky bag of water.

"Nearly there," I reassure her. "One or two more pushes. You are about to meet your baby." As we wait in this strange moment, the baby is visible but not fully out. No longer in, but not yet earthside, between the two worlds. There is a strange quiet as if the world just held its breath.

As the next surge begins, I see the baby start to turn and ready my hands underneath. Mary's knees are bent with each contraction, making her close to the ground but this baby may come at speed and be slippery, I must be waiting. The push begins. Mary acts with the instinct of a thousand generations of labouring women and pushes with a huge roar. The sound fills the space: that powerful sound, the sound that brings babies into the world. As I watch, with a turn of the shoulders, the baby is born, sliding out with the sac intact over its face like a shroud, a gush of the clear waters following behind.

The baby lands in my hands, its fingers reaching, arms outstretched. Waters cascade as Mary sinks with the release.

I feel a shift, like the wind has just suddenly changed direction or when the clouds blow from in front of the moon and the world is lit again. My body feels a shiver but not from fear. It is something else entirely. A sense of enormous peace and love, a presence. For a moment everything pauses as I hold this baby. The world stands still as I gaze at this tiny infant.

"Well done! Well done! Praise God, your baby is here. You did it!" I say, snapping out of the moment. I clear the sac from the baby's face so it can breathe. I have not even looked yet to see whether it is a boy child or a girl. No matter. Mary looks down with a look of absolute amazement on her face and reaches out her hands. I lift the baby straight up into them and she takes the tiny infant up onto her chest, pressing him against her tunic.

The baby does not cry.

When this happens, the Romans will turn them upside down, hang them from their feet and spank them, but my mother said that was a brutal thing to do to a newborn. Instead I watch carefully.

"There are other signs, Salome…" my mother Levona would say. "What colour are they? Are they breathing? Do they move? Only interfere if the baby is not doing those things, otherwise just let them start life gently. Life is hard enough without being smacked at the start."

I can see the baby wriggle and move. Its olive skin looks a healthy colour. The chest rises and falls even with the umbilical cord still attached.

Mary looks at me. Her face, as with the face of all mothers in the seconds after birth, shows both grief and joy at the same time. It flashes with the enormity of the sensations and the pain just endured, and yet at the same time relief, love and elation. This face only lasts a minute or so but it is there at every birth. I keep my watch on the baby, the colour is good, I can see the breathing looks healthy.

Mary is standing, clutching her newborn, blood on her tunic, legs bare and wet where the waters have washed down her, taking the desert dust in streaks with them. She is raw, fragile and quite surprised it is done.

"Well done," I say, holding her arm and meeting her eyes. "You were so strong, Mary." She nods, unable to speak, and almost unsure what to do next. Now she has birthed I must get her to the ground. Many women feel faint after birth and as I am on my own with her, I would struggle with her and the baby if she collapsed. I help her step backwards, still tightly hugging her baby and onto a clean pile of hay as I pull up her tunic to prevent the blood staining it. The hay must scratch a bit, but it is all I have to sit her on.

Once she and the baby are down, I grab the basket ready to catch the placenta. Talking all the time to her, and watching for signs that she is not losing too much blood, I help her lift her tunic off so she can put her baby to the breast. We are now behind the low wall, so even if someone comes in, she is hidden. The baby looks healthy in her arms. The gush of waters that followed had cleared most of the blood from its tiny body leaving the skin shiny. I sit Mary back and help her place the little one near her breast, supporting the head with her arm. It's warm in the stable, but even so I lay her tunic across the baby and Mary's front, as lovingly as if she were my own daughter. Mary suddenly pulls the baby back from her chest slightly and just checks, "It's a boy!" she says as if she is confirming what she already knew before drawing him back to her. "Jesus, his name is to be Jesus."

"Jesus," I repeat, "a lovely name. I have a cousin called Jesus and he is one of my favourite people. It means God is salvation doesn't it?" Mary nods. I'm curious that she is so sure of the name, without any discussion with Joseph. Perhaps they had agreed it already if it was to be a boy. Mary lays back still slightly dazed as new mothers often are, and watches in amazement as the baby opens his eyes and looks quietly at her. This is a most sacred moment, where the baby meets their mother for the first time. After a good birth babies are wide awake and ready to connect, a window of awareness that may not come again for days or even weeks if missed.

I glance down between her legs, checking blood loss, as water and blood dribble slowly from her onto the hay. I sit back on my heels, skirts hitched up off the floor and watch it trickle through the hay and into the earth. I don't want to break the spell between her and her baby. At some point I will check her stomach, check there is no second baby and feel that it is doing what it should, but for now I just watch. The baby Jesus and Mary are quietly drinking each other in, transfixed in each other's gaze. Mary's face, so surprised after the birth, has softened into a smile, she is glowing. I remain quiet while they gaze at one another, Mary stroking his head as if she had been a mother all her life.

Gradually, the baby starts to sense the closeness of the breast and starts to open his mouth, rooting for that first breastfeed. "He is ready to feed," I say. "Just hold him close he knows what to do." The baby's head bobs, his mouth opening wide at the touch of her readied nipple, until gradually, with unsteady head movements, the baby Jesus latches on and sinks into a first feed.

"Well done!" I encourage her. "That's perfect." She smiles a grateful smile. New mothers are so sensitive to the words spoken in these early moments, giving them confidence in their own ability is as much my job as the capability I bring. Feeding is good. This will help the placenta to come soon and easily. In the meantime, there, in the quiet of the stable, with the sound of the donkey and the sheep, down in the hay and earth we sit. Mother, baby and midwife, the smell of the birth, fluid and blood mingling with the smell of animals, earth and hay. It is a stillness and a peace like no other. No big celebrations like the birth yesterday, no hugging, no cheering from a waiting crowd outside the door. In fact, Joseph does not even know yet that he has a son and I realise I must go to tell him, in case the silence worries him.

The placenta will not be long, but I feel I have the time to pop out and tell him. I ask Mary's permission, and when she nods, I run to the door and pull it open. Joseph is right outside the door, I can see him clearly as it is brighter outside than I was expecting, his anxious look fading as he sees my smile.

"It's a boy!" I bluster. "A healthy, handsome boy. Mary is fine. She was so strong." I think for an instant that he might embrace me, but he remembers himself and just beams with joy.

"I'll let you know when you can come in." Then I close the door and head back to Mary and the baby. I crouch back down and ask permission to feel the bump. With a nod, Mary allows me and I feel under the baby's bottom to her stomach. All good. I can feel the womb already reducing in size. I check beneath her and there it is, the trickle of blood suggesting the placenta has detached. You need to watch the blood loss. You need to watch the mother. Sometimes there will appear to be no blood flow from the mother but the placenta doesn't come either. It is blocking the way, filling her womb up with blood and you only realise when the colour starts to leave the mother, as she turns grey in front of you. By then her tummy has expanded and she is slipping quietly to her death, drowning from within. Mary's blood loss seems normal and so I encourage her to kneel up to allow the placenta to come out.

"Can you kneel up?" I ask. "It is time for the afterbirth." Mary nods and, holding her baby tight, I put my arms around her and the baby and help her move her legs as trickles of blood mark them with pathways of red. She draws her legs up and leaning on me raises herself into a kneeling position. That is all it takes. I grab the basket and just get it underneath her as, with a small gush, the placenta slides out and into the woven bowl.

In another complicated manoeuvre of mother, baby and attached placenta in its basket, I help her lie down. Her back is against the rough stone wall, the placenta still attached next to the baby in a basket. My heart wrenches for the poor girl. No comforts, no family, no celebrations, not even a cushion to put behind her. Just the stones, hay and hard earth. Mary, however, appears not to have noticed where she is. She is utterly transfixed with her baby, cradling him, stroking his head and leaning in to kiss him. She looks absolutely beautiful. Even with sweaty hair and bloodied legs she radiates joy. I smile with her, and praise her again which makes her look up at me, a look of grief shooting across her face.

"I wish my mother was here," she whispers. "He is so lovely," she says, stroking the baby's head. My heart leaps out for her. I did not mean to remind her of what she does not have – I get close and take her in my arms.

"Bless you," I say. I wonder again what Joseph meant when he said he couldn't leave her. Was she not safe to be left? What could possibly have happened that she had to be brought so far from home, in her condition? I remember what Leah had said about her not expecting the baby to have been born yet, but the baby Jesus certainly does not look as if he has arrived early, he is a good size and strong. He's not born months early, for sure. I have seen those babies, the ones born too soon. I've struggled to help them breathe and feed, sometimes I've held them as life slipped away, this is the danger of being born too early. This baby is not like one of those. Perhaps that is why she is here – to hide the shame of a baby conceived out of wedlock? No matter. There is a mother in front of me that needs a mother, and so I hold her close and we sit together, me holding her tight as if she were my own daughter. Sometimes, in strange times, there are no strangers.

The baby is feeding well and after a while I need to change the hay underneath her. I gather up the bloodied, damp hay and leave it in the corner closest to the door, then put some fresh hay under her. In a while, I will change to rags to catch the blood, but for now I need to keep checking and it is easier when I can see the loss. I could cut the cord now, but there is no rush. It can sit, still connected, in the basket. The first connection between baby and the mother is too often severed the moment the baby crosses over from womb to land. But a cord left, a baby that gets to hold that connection as they adjust to the world, in my experience gets an advantage missed in those whose mother-lifeline is cut immediately.

Mary leans against the wall, baby naked against her bare skin. They are both covered by her tunic but otherwise she too is naked, in the warmth of the stable. Her hair sweeps over her shoulder and sits covering her other breast. I realise I don't even know if she has more clothes and wonder if they have blankets. I take off my shawl, dyed green using nettles and embroidered by Shifra when she was just twelve and I wrap it around her and the baby, covering her legs with her tunic. The basket containing the placenta, still attached to the baby, sits next to her and I can see the base of it slowly changing colour as the blood seeps through.

"Would you like me to get Joseph?" I ask. She nods and I pull myself up on the wall and walk towards the door. As I open the door, a blue light fills my senses. The sun has set, but instead of the usual darkness there is a beautiful glow. The night has been lit with what feels like a full moon … but there is no full moon tonight, just a new moon rising, a sliver of a crescent. Over the tops of the neighbouring buildings, the dark blanket of the sky sits heavy with a million tiny lights, twinkling and mapping the desert night. But around the door to the stable it is strangely bright. I can see Joseph stop his prayers and focus all his attention on me.

"It's so bright out here!" I say, thinking it must have been darker in the stable than I had thought.

Joseph's voice sounds puzzled. "I know, it started just before you came to tell me he was born. It was like the clouds blew over and the light was there, but there was no cloud, just that … "

He breaks off to point up above us and there it is, hanging above us, casting a warm, ethereal light. A star that seems so much bigger and closer than the others and appears to be directly above us. The star everyone has been talking about. It sits above this stable, on top of the hill that is Bethlehem. I am once again overwhelmed by that feeling of peace and a presence. The world pauses as I look up. A stillness. A sense of awe. We stand together for a moment, necks cricked back to drink in the sight.

I can hardly pull my eyes away from the star. Just as so often I stand outside to stare at the moon, marvelling at her light, detail and the pull she seems to exert on me. Benjamin teases me for my running commentary on the moon's journey over its cycle. I am mesmerised by the beauty of the moon: her changing shape as she appears from the darkness as a sliver, and over the days grows to fullness just as a pregnant belly does before disappearing again into the dark. Her light transforming the night from a place of darkness to a world beautifully illuminated in silver, her absence as noticeable as her glow. This star above us now is holding my attention in just the same way, I am completely captivated.

The spell of the light breaks as Joseph moves and we turn towards the door. He ducks slightly as he steps back into the heat and smell of the stable. Now we are back inside, after the fresh night air, the smell of birth, sweat and animals is bracing. Mary and the baby are gazing at each other as she strokes his tiny head, his little body pressed up against her. They are drinking each other in, in the stillness of the night. The mother and baby dyad, a pairing as old as life itself. I hold back, not wanting to disturb this meeting of father and baby and slip back out to stare at the star.

As I look up at the bright light overhead, I think of all the conversations about it being an omen. What can it mean? Why is something that has been heralded as prophetic right above this tiny town on a hill? Surely it should be over a king's palace, over Jerusalem maybe? And yet, here it is. Over our little town. Lighting this sleeping street. Illuminating these sandy rocks, bathing me in ethereal, calming light. I lean back against the wall behind me, close my eyes and let it wash over and through me. It feels beautiful, calming and I find I'm smiling as, after a while, I open my eyes.

I return into the stable, to find the three of them together on the floor. Joseph is sitting close to Mary as she holds the baby tight. Both transfixed by this tiny, alert fresh face, his wide eyes staring up at them, blinking, as if taking in the new world around him. It's a beautiful sight, and they look up at me beaming as I move round to them.

"It's time to cut the cord and wrap him," I inform her, I have my knife in my bag for this task. I always wash it and rewrap it in soft leather after every use. If I didn't have it with me, it would be better to leave the cord to fall off itself than make a baby ill with an unclean knife. Using plaits of the red thread from my kit, I tie two knots in the cord a short distance from each other. Now the cord is white, there is no danger to the baby as the bleeding through the cord will have stopped. Using the flame of the lamp to heat and clean the knife once more and laying the cord on a small piece of leather on the ground next to Mary's thigh, I cut it.

Now baby and placenta are separated I can check the placenta. As the starlight is so bright I decide to do it outside. Joseph is there to keep an eye on Mary, even though he cannot touch her. I take the basket out of the door and, squatting down low, check the placenta. I need to make sure it's complete or the mother may yet bleed to death. It is still warm as I lift and hold it, gently teasing the folds to check its form. Blood trickles down my fingers as this life-giving miracle tells me its secrets. By the colour and size, I get clues as to whether there was a problem in the pregnancy. If it is not all there, if a part remains inside the mother, it is my sign that she will not stop bleeding. Then I must urgently use whatever I have, such as clary sage, nettle, raspberry leaf, the flower or leaf of the shepherd's purse, basil leaves in hot water, or a few drops of the oil of white lupinus, combined with belly massage to shift the retained parts. There are so many herbs and remedies we have to help us.

Massage, herbs and prayers help, but sometimes Death wins. This life-giving organ that a mother grows may be the very thing that kills her. This placenta however looks healthy and complete. I hold it up one last time towards the bright starlight and thank it for its care of the baby and the mother, and for giving all of itself up now the task is complete. All that remains now is to return it to the earth.

I am struck again by the incredible beauty of the light from above. If this star is a sign, it feels like a good one. I sense no danger in the air tonight. Picking up a handful of sand from the ground, I soak up the blood on my palms and brush the sand and blood mixture off with a quick shake of my fingers.

There is still much to do, I bring the placenta just inside the door, it is too tempting for wild dogs and animals to be left unattended.

Shutting the door behind me, I call for Joseph. "Joseph, it is time to bury the placenta, could you please bring me some water?" I hear him get up. Joseph comes over with the jug of water and pours some over my hands over the gutter as I clean off the last of the blood. "The placenta looks healthy. This is good," I reassure him as I see his face look worried when he spots the bloody pile in the basket. "It must be buried tonight. Have you seen any tools in here?"

Joseph nodded, "There is a hoe in the corner. Where shall I go?"

"Just slightly down the hill and to the right – go out past the big boulder, into the field, dig a hole deep enough to cover it well. You go and dig and I will prepare it." Joseph nods and heads off to pick up the hoe from the far corner. The placenta has birth blood on it so Joseph cannot touch it, but he can dig the hole for me.

If this were a rich household, the placenta might be covered with myrrh and wrapped in a fancy cloth before burial. My grandmother told me it was the respect for the placenta that mattered more than the cost of the materials. "It's important to thank it and bury it with herbs and good thoughts," she would say. I look through my bag for some fragrant smelling herbs.

"The placenta looked healthy and complete," I reassure Mary. "I have thanked it for its work. Now, how are you feeling?" She looks well. She has a good colour but is, as many women are after birth, very quiet.

"I'm a bit sore but isn't he amazing," she says looking down at him. "He's so perfect and so...normal!" I am about to laugh as that is such an odd thing to say, why would a baby not look normal? I stop myself, just in time, words matter at this vulnerable stage after birth.

"He's beautiful," I reassure her.

I dig in my bag, "Found them!" I exclaim as I pull out a small wrap of rose petals and rosemary and return to the door, respectfully placing some on the top of the placenta and thanking it again. It will be buried in the basket with the petals on top.

Now the baby has had a first feed, it is time to clean and wrap him. I bring out another small leather wrap. Each of my wraps contain different herbs, and are marked with a small symbol so I know what they contain. You never know when you will need chamomile to calm a mother, or lavender to slow a fast heartbeat, or clary sage to help to expel a placenta.

At home Benjamin has made me decorated wooden boxes for storing each herb, and from which – after every birth – I restock my bag. The herbs and their uses were taught to me by my mother and grandmothers. They taught me where to find them, how to grow and use them, and when best to harvest them. "Never, in the no moon time, best in the full moon," my grandmother, Mariah, would say. I have passed this wisdom on to my daughters and they will to theirs.

A second wrap, its leather super soft from handling, is filled with salt. Salt has always been such a part of our world. It is how we preserve food, part of our rituals, and part of our protection against evil.

Every newborn is rubbed with salt, to protect and clean them. Sometimes the salt is rubbed straight on, sometimes mixed with water, and sometimes with olive oil. While some midwives rub salt all over the baby, I had learnt from my grandmothers to use the smallest amount, as babies who were rubbed all over would become dried inside and produce dark urine.

"Do you have a swaddling cloth for him?" I ask Mary. "We need to salt and wrap him."

She nods in response and points at her travelling pack. "It's in there, Salome." This is interesting. Leah said they had not expected the baby yet, and Joseph had said that it was not safe to leave her behind. I had at first wondered if they had not known how close they were. But having a swaddling cloth shows that there was some preparedness for this event. For midwives, understanding the situation sometimes takes some working out. Things are not always as they seem.

Mary's travel roll is leaning up against a wall, it's a small roll of grey fabric, filled with her possessions. It contains another two or three rolled up tunics, some head scarves, a leather pouch, a comb, a tiny rolled up swaddling cloth in pale fabric and a pretty weave roll.

"This?" I hold up what looks like the swaddling cloth and Mary nods. The swaddling cloth is another part of our rituals around birth. Birth is honoured and sacred, the role of the midwife is to help at the birth, care for the mother but also to bring the baby into the world with gentleness, observing the important rituals with respect and love for this new life. Welcoming, washing, and wrapping the newborn child are some of these crucial sacred tasks.

Usually, a swaddling cloth is as wide as a woman's hand, from the tip of the fingers to the wrist and about ten times the length of a woman's arm. While some cloths are plain, very often they would be embroidered during the pregnancy with the signs of the family tribe, or religious symbols. I unfurl the soft fabric and I see a small, embroidered lion of the House of David, in a pale purple thread. It has been painstakingly executed, and around the feet of the lion there are leaves and branches that continue across the length of it. It is a real work of love.

"This is exquisite," I say as I sit down beside Mary with the salt and swaddling in my hands. "Did you make it?"

She nods. "I started weaving the cloth the day I knew he was coming. Joseph suggested the lion of the House of David as it's his heritage and why we are here – he drew it out for me to sew."

It is an important signal. Joseph had claimed this child as his own by putting his family mark on this special cloth. If the baby was conceived out of wedlock, he did not have to do that. Before I take Jesus to clean and wrap him, I ready a cloth to rest the baby on right next to Mary so she can help without moving. I place the salt close to her, along with some rosemary I have in my bag, a cloth to wash and another cloth to dry him. I put the swaddling cloth within reach. Finally, I place a drink and a piece of my sweet fruit bread next to Mary for her to eat, now her hands are free.

"Is it okay if I take him now, Mary?" I ask. Some people will just take the baby from the mother, forgetting that while, yes, this ritual needs to be performed, you are separating a duo that have been joined for three seasons, since the moment the baby came into existence. This should be a sacred moment. Gently she lifts him up to me, kissing his head as he is passed up.

It's my first cuddle with him as he's been in his mother's arms since he was born, enjoying her closeness, smell, and love. While I've been watching him closely at first, then every few minutes as he adjusted to life outside of the womb, this is my first proper meeting with him. I tenderly pick him up and cradle his tiny little naked body close to mine. With the first separation from his mother his tiny arms fly up and I think he might cry, but I shush and cradle him, jigging him to soothe him, and whisper welcome prayers into his ear. He settles quickly and watches me with big dark eyes as I lay him down on the cloth. First, I use a wet cloth to wash him down, removing any blood and fluid left on him. Mary holds a reassuring hand on his chest, then head, and hushes him. I dry him off with the second, small piece of cloth, going carefully round the cord which is still white and long and tied.

So often this is a moment of big gestures and ritual, but tonight, here in the dark, sitting in the dirt, the world seems to hush as I offer Mary the open pouch of salt and she takes a small pinch of grains. I leave the open pouch close, as I reach for the small jug of oil. It was very thoughtful of Leah, who, even though she has not given birth, knows the rituals. Jesus lies with his curled-up legs drawn up as if still in utero, but he is amazingly calm. I start the prayer.

May God bless you and keep you;
may God make His face shine upon you and be gracious
to you;
may God lift up His countenance and give you peace.
May the Lord answer you when you are in distress;
may the name of the God of Jacob protect you.
May he send you help from the sanctuary
and grant you support from Zion.
May he remember all your sacrifices
and accept your burnt offerings.
May he give you the desire of your heart
and make all your plans succeed.
May we shout for joy over your victory
and lift up our banners in the name of our God.

I am joined in the quiet prayer by Mary. It is a song of blessing and thanks to God for this baby, a petition to love and protect them both, cleanse them and be with them, a heartfelt request that they may always be held in the hand of God.

Mary ever-so-carefully circles the salt and oil around his chest, watching as this tiny rib cage rises and falls with each breath. I begin on his legs, from the feet to the middle, bringing the salt mixture up, always up. Head, arms, and then our hands swoop underneath him ensuring he is rubbed all over. He is so small and our hands seem so huge. It does not take long and once done we start the swaddle, wrapping him, round his head and down his body, right to his feet, the Lion of Judah displayed at the front, marking him as a child of the House of David. He is held tight, just as he would have been in the womb, and while he will not wear these for long, as his lower part must be free for expulsions, this is an important ritual to have been performed.

It is done. He has been cleaned and claimed as a wanted child, purified with salt and wrapped with love. A look of relief and contentment sweeps over Mary but I notice that she moves as if in some discomfort and my attention returns to her needs.

Now it is time for the cleaning and wrapping of Mary. Joseph has returned, so I ask him to take the baby while I attend to her. He takes baby Jesus in his arms, standing, gently rocking him. His tall frame makes the baby look so incredibly small as he sways, strokes and coos to the tiny life in his arms. He moves closer to the door, lovingly holding his newborn son, so I can wash down Mary's body with some privacy. I can hear him talking softly to baby Jesus in the stillness of the night. It is late now, and the sounds of people have gradually fallen away, but every so often we hear some noise from the road outside: a shout, a dog bark, or a gust of wind.

I have some cleaned balls of smoothed wool for this washing in my bag, but first I will use water and rags to remove the blood and sweat, then wash and purify her with the wool, water, and herbs, finally rubbing on some fragranced oils to cleanse and restore. This is a tradition observed since our days in the red tents and is, in my mind, a most beautiful thing. It is a precious way of honouring the body after it has just brought forth life. A woman is so open after birth. It's a holy, vulnerable time, she's often worn out and as weak as a kitten. She must be treated with gentleness and care. I kneel down next to Mary with the bowl of water for washing, and a small square of cloth to clean her.

I have rose, chamomile, mint, and nettle, each in their small goat skin pouch in my kit. Each plays a different role: rose for cleansing, mint for invigorating, chamomile flowers for soothing. There are so many uses for the plants found all around these hills.

I mix rose into the water and start from her face, neck and shoulders working down her body, cleansing the sweat and dust that have mingled on her skin. By the time I reach her feet, her skin has dried and I start again from the head. This time as a restorative after the cleanse, I massage her body with olive oil infused with basil, especially around the womb. It has worked so hard and now must be treated with care. It must be oiled and touched to make sure it is contracting back and sitting where it should be.

When I am finished, I will bind her belly. I'll wrap a length of cloth tightly around her hips and belly, bringing balance and support to the table of her body, preventing problems in her womb and back later. It takes time as I am doing it on my own. Baby Jesus still full and content from the first feed is settled well in his father's arms. I feel, after the journey to get here, Mary needs the time and care.

We don't speak much as I clean her and begin to massage her body. I have learnt the value of silent care when women are in this stage. They have just stepped through the fire of birth, they have opened up to bring life, and are now open, raw and otherworldly. This is not a time for idle chat. Sometimes a woman will want to talk, the energy of birth still flooding out. Mostly at this point they need to be allowed to sit in this space, like a warrior after a battle, exhausted, reflective and appreciating that they have survived to win such a prize.

I move from head to toe with the massage. In big sweeping movements, light in pressure, helping to shift all that has been retained and is no longer needed after the birth. These big strokes help refresh and soothe her entire body, head to feet. After this I return to her middle to work on the womb, the incredible life-giving space we women hold inside.

The belly massage is the most important part of this post-birth rite. It soothes the womb, helps release the blood, and makes sure all is returning to place. It has been through such a monumental change. It has worked so hard to grow and birth this baby. Even just its monthly clearing of itself shows how much power it holds

THE BIRTHKEEPER OF BETHLEHEM

in the strength of the sensations. After birth, it is open to infection and problems of healing if not properly cared for, so this is not just a ritual of respect, but protection as well. When women miss this ritual, I've observed that their recovery is slower, and they risk more healing problems, both physically and spiritually.

Placing my hands on her still large belly, I begin by circling, gradually bringing the circle into the centre, before moving to the outside and back, circling into the centre. I use the palm of my hand to lead, pulling gently into the middle like the sun's rays, moving towards the centre of her being. It both thanks and restores the womb. Today, I am super light in my touch, but this should ideally be repeated every day for forty days, and the pressure will gradually build up over the time.

Once this is done, I go to my bag and find a tightly rolled-up weave, to wrap her belly and hold her womb tight. Mary, seeing what I am getting, speaks up, "Salome, I have one in my bag. It was made for me by my cousin Elizabeth. She has just had her first child – in her older years," she smiles.

This is so good to hear, that she has someone who has celebrated this birth with her. The picture is gradually building. Leah had said the baby was not expected for a long time and yet this baby did not look at all early: he is too big and too ready. It would explain why she had come with Joseph. Why she had risked herself and her baby on such a painful journey so close to her birth time. Terrible things sometimes happen to mothers who fall pregnant outside of marriage. Abandonment is common, public shaming, as well as the killing of mother and baby. It all makes more sense now, why Leah's husband did not want them in the house. It must be a cause of great shame to the family. But I love my friend Leah even more for standing her ground, protecting this couple and making as lovely a space as she could for them.

I go to her rolled mat and find a tightly wrapped weave. It is beautifully made and a delicate pale blue, most likely made from a dye from the flowering alkanet plant. There is a pattern to the weave, diagonals of lighter and darker wool. "Oh, this is beautiful – clearly made with much love for you," I remark as I hold it up and run the soft wool through my fingers. I kneel back down beside her, gently unravelling it as I reach around her and wrap it round her still swollen belly. Round and tight, not painfully tight, but supportive, holding the womb space together as her body recovers from the huge loss it has just experienced. For that is how a womb always feels to me just after a birth. This space that has grown and nurtured, fed, warmed and cared for a baby is suddenly left bereft, empty and bleeding. No wonder we must care for new mothers. For a short while, they are wide open and raw.

I reach round and wrap, round and wrap, round and wrap, starting low on her belly and rising up over her now empty bump. As I do, I quietly pray for this woman, this baby. I give thanks for the baby's safe arrival, for sparing the mother, for once again being allowed to witness such holiness, for that is how it feels to me. This is the moment of connection to the hand that made us all. It feels like the love and thoughts that I have while I wrap her will be infused in the cloth, so the wrap must never be rushed or rough. It is a holy act. I take my time and pour blessings into mother and child as I go. Finally reaching the end, I tuck the finish tightly and smile at Mary.

"There, that will hold you tight as your body recovers." The wrap is firm enough to support but will not restrict her movement. Carefully I help her to stand, she is a bit shaky and fresh blood trickles down her cleaned legs.

"Just hold the wood while I change the hay, Mary," I say, indicating that she should support herself while I quickly gather up the blood-soaked hay from underneath her, and put fresh down. Then, as if dressing a child, I help pull her tunic over her head, and lower her back to sit again covering her legs with a cloth. It is easier to let the blood flow to the ground when we have so few spare clothes.

Now she is wrapped, she must eat and drink to restore her strength. She is still in danger until the bleeding stops. It may be days, even weeks away. She must rest and be taken care of.

I pass her a glass from the table, and from my bag find the goatskin pouch of the wine, raspberry leaf, honey and chamomile mix, and pour her a glass. "Drink this. It will help you feel more comfortable and give you strength." I pass her some of the sweet bread – flat bread baked with raisins, berries, honey and herbs, the warming taste of sage as a background to the sweet jewels of fruit. It is both delicious and full of goodness to nourish and strengthen her.

The placenta needs to be buried, so I suggest we put the baby in the manger for a minute while Joseph takes me to the hole he has dug. We call him back in and he returns, having stepped outside to, in his words, "Show his son the bright star that was there as he was born." He is beaming with delight as he holds the now sleeping baby.

"Come and show me where you dug this hole, Joseph. I will bring the placenta and we can bury it," I say. "But we must be quick. Mary should not be left alone long at this point." He nods in agreement and very carefully lowers the peaceful infant into the stone-carved manger. The soft sheepskin makes a padded protection between him and the coarse surface. Joseph tucks the tiny, swaddled baby in with such care. I tidy my head scarf, pick up the basket containing the placenta, and follow him into the night.

CHAPTER FOUR

Shepherds

We walk quickly and quietly, lit by the star and following the road out of the town. Ahead of us is a scattering of trees, mostly olive but there are also some gall oak, and redbud. The dusty earth is darkened with the occasional shrub or bush as the ground slopes down the hill and into the night where it joins the rise and fall of the mountains.

The placenta would usually be buried in the garden or yard of the house, but this is not their home. In ancient times more importance had been placed on where it was buried (near water to ensure access to water throughout life, on a mountain for strength, in a sand dune for resilience) but when our people had been in the desert sometimes the choice was not ours to make and those symbolic connections had been lost, although thankfully not the importance of returning the placenta to the ground.

"It took a little while," says Joseph, his voice cheerful, "as I wanted to find the right place. Being so far from home, where the placenta is to rest feels meaningful. I'm a carpenter, so wood is my craft and my life. It has to be by a tree and the right one at that."

I turn to look at him in wonder, "My husband Benjamin is a carpenter as well!" I laugh, "Another man who feels the same way about wood – he will like you!"

"I'd like to meet him!" said Joseph as we work our way through the

86

field. "I checked each tree until I found it. Here it is. Not too old, not too young, I was looking for a strong root and branch, healthy leaves and fruit." From somewhere I get a feeling that this couple will be more to me and my family than just strangers I helped.

Ahead of us is a solid, gnarled olive, reaching its arms up and out as if greeting the starlight. Its fine branches are made of healthy wood, and its tipped leaves offer a blue hue against the bark. The starlight from above gives it a complete shadow underneath, a dark mirror image on the ground. As above, so below.

"Olive is the wood I work with the most. Beautiful, lined and so adaptable to creation," Joseph says admiring it. Next to it, he has dug a small neat hole. Carefully I lower the placenta in, thanking it one last time for its service. Then I stand back admiring the stars as he covers it back in. He is about to continue talking when I nudge him. We are being watched.

Three men had emerged from the shadows of some rocks and are standing in a group talking in an animated fashion and watching what we are doing. It is only their crooks that reassure us that they are shepherds, and not robbers or bandits. I can see them discussing something between them – hands gesturing and the sound of low voices carrying in the night.

After a minute or so something was clearly agreed between them and, led by the older of the three, they walk towards us. Each wears the traditional long tunic, tied with cord at the waist, on top of which is a dark grey cloak. Their heads are covered but I recognise their weathered faces as Shepherds of the Tower. The most elderly of them is Uziel, the head of the shepherds, but I don't understand what's going on or why they are here in the dead of night.

As they draw close, Uziel says, "Greetings, Mother Salome. May God's blessing be on you and your family." He bows slightly to me, as I do to him. He turns to Joseph, "Blessings upon you stranger. My name is Uziel, this is Shay, and Natan." He indicates the two younger men with him. "We are the shepherds of the flock of Migdal Eder. What are you doing out here tonight?"

Joseph replies, "I am Joseph of Nazareth, my wife has just given birth and I was burying the afterbirth as we are not in our home." A look shot between the three men.

"Tonight? The baby was born tonight?" one asks. Joseph nods, unsure why this was being asked.

"Yes, just as the stars joined."

The older man, his leathery hands grasping the staff of his hook, takes a deep breath and continues. "We had a vision...a visitor came to the three of us, and told us that a child would be born tonight, a child who will be of great importance, and that we were to pay him homage. He said a man would come to us and show us the way to the child. I ask you to do that so we may see this baby."

Our shock must have been palpable, as Uziel quickly reassures us, "We felt the same when the stranger spoke to us, but he said to us, 'Do not be afraid.' Do not be afraid, Mother Salome, Joseph of Nazareth. We are men of the flock and men of God. We understand the signs and this is God's wish."

I cannot imagine what is happening or why. Men do not attend the newborn of a stranger! What connection do these men have to this child, and what does he mean he had a vision? But these men are no ordinary shepherds, they are the holy men of Migdal Eder and so I cannot refuse them. Despite our surprise and confusion at this turn of events, Joseph and I lead the men back to the stable.

It is now very late, most of Bethlehem is sleeping. The night sky is still lit by the bright star. As we get to the door, I ask for a moment to make sure Mary is covered, before they enter.

I go in, wondering what I am going to tell her. Shutting the door behind me, I cross the stable and go behind the partition to where

Mary sits, in the semi-darkness. She is sitting quietly, one hand on the infant Jesus, just staring at him. So often you see this after birth. Women, who should be exhausted after all the work they have been through to meet their baby, will then sit up all night watching or talking to these new tiny beings.

"Mary, there are holy shepherds here from the Tower of the Flock. They want to see the baby," I say, my confusion apparent.

Her face, that had been so relaxed after the massage and wrapping, suddenly looks a bit scared. "What has brought them here?" she asks. And then, as if she realises something, she just quietly replies, "As it must be," and asks me to help her.

I help Mary pull her tunic down and wrap her hair up in her scarf, smoothing out her clothes and making her look as respectable as I can. She wants to stand to greet them, but I will not allow it: she has just given birth and I cannot risk her losing too much blood. I squeeze her hand, smile at her and we call them to enter. The baby Jesus lies oblivious to the activity, wrapped tightly in swaddling blankets, eyes open as he looks up from the manger.

The three shepherds and Joseph enter, ducking through the low doorway, eyes adjusting to the dark. The smell of the stable has been sweetened by the herbs I'd used when I massaged Mary's belly, but it is still mixed with the undeniable smell of sweat and birth.

On seeing Jesus swaddled, with the lion of Judah clearly displayed on his front, fast asleep in the makeshift crib, Uziel kneels. Shay and Natan follow quickly behind. Has the star sent everyone crazy? Why are these holy shepherds in here kneeling before a baby? In all my years, I have never seen anything like it.

Uziel looks at Mary. "Blessings on you woman. We pay homage to this child. We were told of his coming."

"Thank you," she replies in a quiet voice. "We are very honoured that you have come to mark his arrival." My bewilderment must have shown, as Uziel looks at me, his face turning quite serious.

"Mother Salome, this child's coming was foretold. We knew when the stars started to move together. The land has been giving us signs. We knew it was tonight. We shepherds know how to read the signs, just as you do as a midwife. Scripture tells us of a child to be born of the House of David, referred to as the Lamb, and then we saw a messenger who told us a man would lead us to him. That was when you and Joseph appeared. You led us here to see the baby wrapped, as we wrap those lambs destined for the temple in Jerusalem. This is not by chance, Salome. Take care of this family. This child has our blessing. Anything you need for his care, do not hesitate to come to me."

I nod, too surprised and confused to think. Once again I remember that sense I'd had as the waters had broken and the baby moved to our world. That feeling of a huge presence of goodness, of peace and power combined in an instant.

The men stand up, and taking their leave, depart, leaving the three of us wondering what just happened. I notice Mary and Joseph exchange a long, loaded look. It took me a moment to think what I was going to do next. The answer was simple. Do what I always did – care for the mother and the new baby. That never changes.

"You give the same care…" my mother would say, "…whether princess or pauper. We are all the same in God's eyes and no one is more in need of care than a woman who has just given birth."

I will talk to Benjamin about what had happened when I get home but right now it makes no sense. How could this baby, born in such lowly circumstances, be so special? I decide that if Mary and Joseph want to share more with me they can, but they had looked as surprised by the visit as me. I notice they both look exhausted. I feel exhausted. We need to get everyone to settle, as it will not be long before the baby needs to feed again, and so we all need to sleep.

It is not allowed for Joseph to sleep near Mary while she is still bleeding, so, after saying goodnight to her and the baby, he takes his roll over by the door. I help settle Mary back down for a sleep and lie down next to her. It is too late to go home on my own and I do not want her left alone for any length of time. At first light, if all is well, I will go home and get Shifra or Martha to take my place here.

Very soon, the baby starts to snuffle for a feed and quickly I get up and pick him up. I unwrap him from the swaddle and hold him over the drain. As the colder air hits him, his bladder empties in a small shower into the earth, ensuring he will not now wee on Mary as she feeds him. Meanwhile, Mary has pulled herself up to a sitting position, and opened her top for him. I pass him over and put him on her chest for a feed, his tiny bare body next to her skin. I help her get him latched, seeing her wince during the first few seconds of him taking hold.

This is very common in the first days, so I squeeze her arm supportively and lock eyes with her, reassuring her with whispered words. These initial feeds can produce very sharp pains that won't last, but need to be endured. Once he is on and the gentle sound of him swallowing can be heard, I go and pour a drink for Mary, offering her a piece of sweet bread to nibble as well. Once again, we feel like the only people awake in the world; mother, baby, and midwife, marking the tiny hours of newborn life and the introduction to the new way of being. Once he is fed, I show her how to hold him to let the milk settle before they both lay back to sleep together. All the time, I'm watching for the twitching that shows he is about to empty his bowels.

Especially when my people were in the desert, washing clothes was a luxury and so we became skilled at spotting the signs and holding a baby out for wee and poo. It is easy enough once you work out your baby's signals, it just takes practice. Sure enough, the face crunching and twitching comes, we hold him out and the dark green first poo is passed safely into the drain.

The feed has caused a gush of blood as her womb closes back down and so I again swap some meadow grass from beneath her for fresh hay (we will need to gather some more tomorrow) and settle down to nap close to her as she sleeps curled up around the baby. I say a prayer of thanks and, even though it is not far off dawn, wish Benjamin a goodnight. He is used to me not making it home, or creeping in late at night. Wherever I am though, I wish him goodnight in my heart and then fall asleep on the hard floor.

CHAPTER FIVE

The Forty Days

For the first forty days, I visit Mary daily. Tending to her, bringing nourishment, massaging her belly, re-wrapping her, helping her master the art of breastfeeding, and learn about mothering her little one. She is an absolute delight with him. She and Joseph both are. They are always cuddling and kissing him, chatting, singing him songs. Mary carries him with her whenever she moves – his tiny form bound to her body in a big shawl.

Mary is still not to do any manual labour, but she does sit and sew when Jesus sleeps. They had stayed in the stable for the first eight days, then – as some of the guests left Leah and Gad's, and now Mary is out of the initial post-birth period – they were able to move into a guest room in the house.

Leah had been at the door first thing in the morning after the birth. I'll never forget the utter wonder on her face as she held the baby for the first time, her usually distracted face softening to the most heart-warming smile as she held and rocked the tiny baby and whispered the most loving welcome and prayers into his ears.

While she had never been blessed with her own child, her heart had not hardened like some who are so cruelly rendered barren. It takes so much from those women, not being able to cross the threshold to motherhood and so robbing them of status in our society. I do not know why God will bless some women with wombs that make healthy babies as easily as a tree grows fruit, and some that cannot bring life forth. It seems such a cruel unfairness.

Despite all her demands at home and taking care of all of her guests, during those eight days Leah comes out whenever she can to help Mary and see Jesus. She even sends food and pays a boy from the village to gather fresh meadow hay every day. It is she who organised the *brit milah,* circumcision, for Jesus in accordance with tradition. To everyone's surprise, the morning of the *brit milah,* a lamb arrives for the celebration from Uziel, a gift from the shepherds.

I have learnt to spend that day with the mother, caring for her as she has to hand her baby over for possibly the first time. Mothers are still so raw and vulnerable at this point. They are often quite lost without their babies in their arms and, not always, but most often, moved to the core by the sound of their baby crying. While all focus is on the baby, I stay with the mother and count the time with her until she has her baby back in her arms and on her chest.

It is at the end of this forty day period that I get confirmation around my suspicions about why Mary was on the road so close to her delivery date.

Leah and I are letting Mary rest. I had massaged Mary's belly as I did every day, and left her wrapped-up and sleeping, while we cared for the baby. Although Leah is usually there when I do this, I hadn't realised how difficult this sometimes is for her. Her willingness to look after Mary meant I had missed her sorrow and her sense of loss. A few days earlier I had offered to teach Leah how to massage Mary and she had refused too quickly, too absolutely, before covering with reasons of preferring to hold the baby. While she feels so much love for Mary and the baby, it is a step too close to the wound for her to touch a recently pregnant belly when hers has never been able to gift her a much longed-for child.

I'd finished the massage and was putting my oils away, as Leah sits close, rocking an alert Jesus and singing songs to him. "We've decided they shall stay here," she tells me and then her voice drops to a whisper. "If they go home now, the family will be shamed. They will stay here with me till the baby is old enough for no one to know his age. There was great upset when it was discovered she was pregnant." She looks at me as if weighing up whether I can be trusted with something.

"The thing is, Salome, perhaps there is something more. Mary swore she had not lain with a man…but she knew she would have a boy and he was to be called Jesus. Joseph was all set to divorce her, when he also had a dream, one that changed his mind." She pauses, stroking Jesus' dark hair, "No one of course believed her, but the shepherds…I cannot explain the shepherds. Why would they come and say such a thing?" She looks at me, eyes demanding an answer. "If they were ordinary shepherds I might have thought they had been paid to say such a thing. Perhaps by Joseph, being kind to save his wife's shame. But the Shepherds of the Tower are honourable holy men. They would not risk their reputation. It makes no sense…" She trails off, lost in thoughts.

So that is why he could not leave her, that is why she had to make that long arduous journey, and risk herself and the baby. Being left behind held more dangers. I have no idea what to say. What would she think if I told her of the sensation I'd had when he was born? That absolute feeling of the presence of something, something more and good. Then the shepherds coming as if to confirm that. And yet… outside of the unusual circumstances around his birth, everything could not be more normal. He was just a baby, and they were lovely, but completely ordinary loving parents. There was nothing about the family that suggested why a star and holy shepherds could have featured in their story.

In fact, now the curiosity of the visit from the shepherds has died down, everything has returned to normal. Here we are at the end of the forty days and Joseph and Mary have become part of everyday life. Joseph had offered to pay for my services with either money or in kind with his carpentry. As business was busy, it was decided Joseph would help Benjamin and Eitan. He has proved to be quite skilled for such a young man and Benjamin has taken him under his wing and employed him. I visit Mary most days and we have become very close. She is a lovely, gentle soul. And Jesus is a just baby, a beautiful, loved baby.

It's all so ordinary that the words of the shepherds seem like a strange dream, a weird occurrence brought on only by the magic of the star.

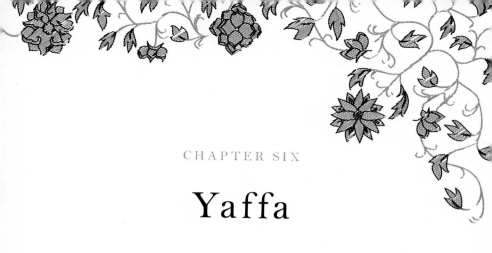

CHAPTER SIX

Yaffa

Over a year has passed since that night when the stars joined. The crops have grown and been brought in, children once again surprised everyone as their limbs stretched, as if we didn't expect them to grow up. Babies have been born and members of our community died. The wheel of life has turned and turned again.

Joseph and Mary have become part of our lives, Joseph working together with Benjamin and Eitan, and Mary visiting us with Jesus at least twice a week. Mary has become very close to both me and my girls, she is lovely company, wise beyond her years, joyful and always willing to lend a hand. She often helps with the children in the courtyard when the pregnant women come to see me, organising games and songs that make the space come alive. It's not just that, her empathy and kindness are beyond her years. I often find her sitting and talking with women who need an ear. She seems to know who needs extra care and gives it with gentleness and sympathy. Jesus has grown from a babe in arms to crawling and now he is beaming as he takes tentative, tottering steps around his mother.

Women have come and gone from our courtyard, bellies rocked, emotions soothed, both herbs and comfort given. One of those women is the lovely Yaffa.

Yaffa had become pregnant within a few moons of seeing me.

However, while she usually birthed easily, this one is proving harder work. The baby – which had been perfectly positioned all the way through pregnancy – has moved. Unlike the previous five births, this one is slow and painful, the contractions while strong, just don't seem to be effective.

Martha has come with me, I know it is one of the last births we will attend together before she is married. I like her fiancé Gideon, he's the son of a friend of Benjamin and a lovely young man, but I'm feeling this imminent loss keenly. It feels both special and a little heart-breaking to me. Yaffa, expecting another quick birth, had called us as soon as she felt the first contractions early this morning, but now as evening falls on this birth it is becoming apparent that the contractions are not moving things on. The excited mood in the room has turned to watchful observance.

Both Martha and I have pressed our heads against her tummy in between the tightenings and thankfully the heartbeat sounds good, but still the labour is not progressing.

As darkness falls and lamps are lit, our observance turns to quiet concern. A feel of the tummy suggests that baby is lying with their head tipped back, when it should be tucked in. While a baby can eventually be born this way, it can be a long process, too often leaving damage to mother in the form of tears and harm to the rear passage. Some women labour for days, and by the time the infant is born, the mother has lost control of her bowel movements. Life for those women is destroyed, the social stigma and trauma of it crippling their lives. Some babies will correct their position on their own and time should be given to see whether the body resolves this itself. But in this case, there are other signs that this baby is stuck. Yaffa seems swollen below and when Martha inserts a finger to feel the baby's head, Yaffa feels dry inside, all indications that the baby is in a bad position. Without fixing this we could lose or damage the baby and cause untold harm to Yaffa.

It was Martha who suggested it, she has grown in confidence since she met Gideon. I think it is being seen in her own right, as more than just as my daughter that has helped. "Shall we try a reposition?" she says to me. "I think the head is not tucked in."

"I think so too, go ahead," I nod. My mother, Levona, had gradually done the same for me, standing back and letting me lead, watching, and perhaps gently guiding, but allowing my confidence to grow with a safe pair of eyes behind me.

Martha turns to Yaffa, "Your baby is not coming down as we would like. We need to help it reposition itself, is that okay?" Yaffa nods in silence, already tired out from a day of contractions. She has birthed enough times to know that this is not as it should be. "What we need to do," Martha explains, "is to move the baby back up and let it come back down into the pelvis in a better position." Yaffa nods but does not speak as another contraction starts. I watch her close her eyes and, sitting on the carved birthstool, rock her way through it.

Martha turns to Yaffa's oldest daughter Zemira, who has started her blood-time and so is able to attend the birth, "Do you have a low table?" Martha's voice is quick but kind, "Go get it, take your aunt to help." While still young, Zemira has an old head on her shoulders, she nods and disappears taking a small wiry looking aunty with her.

They return noisily before the next contraction begins, carrying between them a low sturdy table, occasionally knocking things as they manoeuvre into the room. Four solid legs hold a rectangular flat slab of wood, beautifully smooth after years of use as the main table of the household. Usually food would be served up on it as everyone sat on the floor around, games were played on it, crafts, cooking and a lifetime's work done on it. Now it is half lifted, half dragged into the room to help.

First, we put folded blankets on the table which will go under her knees for comfort, then, as the next contraction ends, we ask Yaffa to kneel on the table. Once in position we wait for a gap between contractions. As soon as the break begins, we help her lower herself forward so her arms and head are on the floor and her bottom high in the air. Her bump adjusts to the change in gravity, the shape of it shifting as she leans forward and down.

"Hold it there. Hold it!" Martha instructs, until the first sign of the next contraction when we help Yaffa back upright for the duration of the surge. Once done, we again help guide her back down. Three times this is repeated, and on the last turn, Martha – kneeling down beside her – uses her slender hands to help move the baby. I watch her, my breath held as she feels the shape of the baby, with Yaffa effectively upside down, Martha uses the gentlest pressure to encourage the baby's head out of the pelvis. I watch Martha ever so carefully pushing down just slightly, hopefully giving the baby the space to reposition its head. I notice my own fingers are twitching to help. Then Martha signals to me and we help Yaffa back up on to the birthstool and wait to see if it has worked.

A pensive silence falls over us all. Myself, Martha, Zemira and two female relatives, always affectionately called Aunty, wait. We need this to work.

The trick is to wait and watch, and not to leap in and feel the baby again, potentially frightening them and making them startle back into a difficult position. But it's so hard not to touch, to feel, to check. We need to wait and see what the labour itself tells us. Whether the pattern of contractions can tell us it's worked, whether the baby can reposition itself and move through the pelvis. Martha is clearly itching to check, but I rest my hand on her arm and say as quietly as I can, "Watch and wait, Martha. Watch and wait..."

It takes another three contractions before we start to see that it might just have worked. The shape of Yaffa's bump changes, the contractions start to get stronger and closer together. Daring to hope, we work to reenergise the room. I use my nails to scrape the peel of a fresh lemon, releasing its powerful scent into the room. It sharpens, lifts, and invigorates all who inhale it. One of the aunties is instructed to feed Yaffa small pieces of date. These will help her womb but also help keep her energy up. A brisk rub down of her legs as she sits on the stool helps to reawaken her body and its energy. It is no time before she has an urge to push, and sitting upright on the birth stool she starts to move her baby down with each long breath. Martha kneels in front of Yaffa and checks the baby is descending, she looks up with a smile and a nod, it has worked.

Yaffa's body takes over, it has done this before. She starts to fidget on the birth stool, the position clearly not suiting her any more. She lowers herself onto the floor and onto all fours. This instinctive behaviour is wonderful for helping birth babies. Sometimes a mother will make peculiar moves with her pelvis during contractions, thrusting or leaning back and arching her hips forward. The moves don't make any sense to the observer but then, when the baby is born it will come out with a hand by its head or an unusual moulding in the skull, showing it had been in an awkward position and needed those very moves to navigate its way out. Martha, wisely, does not comment on the change or suggest anything, she lets the wisdom of the body guide this mother through the final stages. On the floor, on all fours, Yaffa draws her knees closer together, pushing her feet further apart. It's done without commentary, just accompanied by deep guttural sounds. This slight change in position opens up the pelvis as we observe the hips widen and the baby descend even further. With the next few surges, at the top of her bottom, a bulge appears, a diamond shape appearing to push up under the skin. This, my grandmother would say, is the mark of the baby descending, it's the baby's head shifting the bones to make room to be born, both mother and baby working together in this dance of birth.

Yaffa is moving herself again, this time she is sitting back onto her heels and raising herself upright. She pauses for a contraction, a hand reaching down to hold the emerging head. Her sounds are powerful and focused, eyes closed as she feels her way through this birth, responding to the calls of her body. As she holds herself, she helps slow the descent of the baby and prevent tearing. I find myself watching once again in awe. It never fails to amaze me how a woman knows instinctively what to do to birth her baby, it is a secret knowledge that we often don't even know we have until we use it. She pulls a knee out to the side, still sitting upright on her heels and breathing small breaths, we watch the head emerge and retreat, emerge and retreat, until with a turn to the side, it is out. With a huge roar, Yaffa pushes again and the baby slides out onto her own hands held just above the floor. Martha is close to her, watching, and I'm impressed she has not moved to interfere. She has the confidence to leave the mother to birth.

Yaffa pauses for a moment, she does not immediately pick the baby up but holds for a moment looking at it, as if memorizing her baby's face and this moment. She gently smiles at her baby, cooing soft welcome noises before scooping it up and onto her chest. I see this so often, a pause after the birth, marking a shift between the worlds of pregnancy and motherhood. The final step of the journey, savoured for just a short while.

"Another girl!" announces Yaffa, as she cuddles her new baby on her chest. "Who will tell my husband I have given him another girl?" She laughs. Her eyes are twinkling with love. "She is very beautiful, look at her. I do make fine strong girls!"

Even though it's not the hoped-for son, this is a family of so much love and I know their newest daughter will be welcomed with joy. This is not always the case. The pressure on women to produce a son is immense. I felt it from my own mother-in-law. A slight disappointment in each girl. The view that boys will stay and work the land or the business, while girls will marry and go their husband's house. I see it over and over again, this pressure to have a boy. It is something of a relief that I cannot use herbs or skills to ensure the sex of a baby. I fear only boys would be chosen.

I lean into Martha and whisper quietly, "You did well. Look at the baby's head, you can see the moulding has a ridge at the front, where she was sitting in the pelvis. Without your actions, she could not have been born." Martha nods, looking pleased, and I feel a surge of pride in my daughter's skills. She is ready: ready to marry, ready to leave the family home and ready to midwife on her own.

We help get Yaffa and the baby into a more comfortable position and watch for signs of the placenta coming. By the sixth baby, it is not uncommon for the placenta to need encouragement, so we offer Yaffa a drink containing herbs known to help the delivery and reduce blood loss. I've heard of people tugging on the cord after birth with disastrous consequences as it can cause uncontrollable bleeding. The placenta can be encouraged with herbs and massage but should not be yanked away.

"Here, Yaffa, drink this," says Martha pouring a small amount into a goblet. "It contains raspberry leaf and shepherds purse to help get your placenta out. And a bit of honey for sweetness and strength."

Yaffa nods and, sitting back holding her baby, takes small sips. The new baby girl bobs her head on the breast and latches on for a first feed, which will also help the womb to contract down and bring out the placenta. It isn't long before a little gush of blood alerts us that it has detached and is ready, with a small push, to come out.

After so many pregnancies, blood loss after the birth can be high, so we stay much longer than usual to make sure she does not lose too much. It seems that every birth a mother has, the more care she needs afterwards. After a first birth, the mother needs help *with* her mothering, after many births, it is the mother who needs mothering.

"I'll bring you a different mix tomorrow, Yaffa," says Martha, "As I'm sure you remember those afterpains can be a shocker, and more so with each baby. We will help you with a mix of herbs to ease the pains."

Yaffa winces slightly at the thought. "Oh yes please, the last ones after Hannah's birth felt worse than the labour."

The uterus starts pregnancy the size of a small pear, but by the time the baby is born it will have grown to over the size of the baby. It will take nearly two moons to contract back to normal. After a first baby it is often not very noticeable as it does this, but with each pregnancy those sensations become increasingly painful. We will make sure in those first few weeks that she has a mix including raspberry leaf, anise, peppermint and chamomile to help the process and soothe the pain.

Many mothers also need our help as with a houseful of children already, they usually begin pregnancy more tired than a woman having her first baby. They need extra nourishment after birth to get back to full health.

I turn to the aunty who had helped bring the table in, "What a good thing you are here to care for her. You must make sure she has lots of the right foods to restore her strength and help breastfeeding. Every day try to include a mix of cabbage, cauliflowers, peppers, mallow and lentils for strength. Fenugreek and oats for milk supply. Use lots of caraway, coriander and fennel as flavourings as they are all a mother's friend at this time." She looks slightly overwhelmed before I add, "Don't worry we will come every day to help, to massage her belly and bring herbal mixes to ensure she recovers well."

We wash Yaffa's skin, clearing away the blood and sweat of birth. Martha then massages her belly, wrapping her with care and prayer, as the aunties salt, oil and wrap the baby. These rituals are so important for healing and marking the customs of our people, but they are also beautiful. Honouring the mother, honouring her body and the work it has done. Binding women together. Women caring for women.

I love the chatter and buzz of the birth room once the baby has arrived. The excitement staying in our bodies for a while, making sure that we are awake and ready to care for the baby and mother until, as it always does, the tiredness and calm come. As it is the early hours of the morning, we decide that the aunties and Zemira should go and rest, while we will stay and take it in turns to watch over Yaffa until it is light and safer to walk home.

I'm woken from my sleep on the floor of the birthroom, by a squeal of delight. Martha is awake next to Yaffa who is being hugged by one of her younger daughters as they are brought in to meet their new sister. I can tell they are trying to be quiet but their excited little hearts just can't manage it. I watch in bleary-eyed delight as little Hannah, whose birth I'd been at not two years before, covers the baby in big toddler kisses and cuddles.

As the aunties take over the morning care, we gather our things and head out into a sunny Bethlehem morning. There's not much chat as we head home, we'd said all we needed to last night in whispers while Yaffa slept. Walking, arms linked in a peaceful silence, I'm reminded of walking home in the dawn the morning after Jesus was born. Martha had arrived as soon as it was light, after they'd woken up and realised I still wasn't back. She'd come to relieve me if the birth was still ongoing. She, too, had gone straight to the house and been directed to the stable where she found us awake and caring for the baby in the most humble of surroundings.

How different it was for Mary compared to this morning. No celebrations, no home comforts, no family. One mother on her first and the other on her sixth birth, one surrounded by family and one with a stranger, but both labouring with the ingrained instinct of a thousand generations.

On the way home we run into Denah. Her baby boy, Arran, now a few months old, is strapped to her front, fast asleep in her big shawl. It is lovely to see her. She has changed, as most women do as they step across the threshold to motherhood. She is now so much more mature than the young woman who had come to me desperate to become pregnant. Being a mother has given her more confidence and she carries herself differently.

Denah's labour had been as smooth as a first birth can be. Like most first-time mothers it had taken longer. The womb, I think, learns each time and does it faster with each birth, but the first time, takes time. She had remained calm and focused in a way I had not expected her to. A stoical girl, she had applied that same strength to birth, not allowing herself to be overwhelmed but constantly taking herself back to a quiet state and riding each wave of birth with resolve. She had roared her baby out on the birthstones with no complications or difficulty.

The baby was born strong and well, and as a boy had brought great joy to her mother-in-law, Hallel. The birth of the grandson and their shared love for him had thankfully, over the forty day period and months that followed, helped unite the two women into a more evenly balanced relationship.

It is a wonderful thing to watch a mother change, especially in those first forty days. From her feeling raw and open, gradually with good food, support, daily massage and wrapping, she emerges at the end of the isolation a different being. She has survived the birth but also been allowed to heal and recover. For forty days she has been surrounded by women there to nourish, help and guide her, giving her confidence in her mothering. She is well equipped by the end of this time to return to the world, not just rested but also more skilled in the delicate art of being a mother.

We hug as we part, delighted to have seen her and the baby.

The forty days ahead with Yaffa will be different to the days we spent with Denah. Yaffa knows how to mother, but her body will need more care, the other children will need support and amusement, but the result at the end will hopefully be the same: a rested, restored and ready mother.

CHAPTER SEVEN

The Magi

So it was until the day the Magi arrived. Nothing was the same after that. Perhaps if they had not come, Herod would never have come for the children of Bethlehem.

But come they did.

Ruth is working her magic on my back, her supple fingers kneading and releasing the tightness I hold in my shoulders. We chat as I sit in front for her, catching up on news as she pummels, strokes and fixes my aches. She is one of my best friends and has been since childhood. Apart from my girls and Benjamin, she was the only one I had told about the strange visit from the shepherds over a year ago now. I can unload all my stories to her, she would no more gossip than a desert rock start talking.

"What have you been doing, Salome? You are as tight as a drum!" Ruth remarks as her fingers probe a tender point in my shoulder.

"The usual," I reply wincing slightly at the heat in my muscle, "up all night with a mother. You know my work, so much is just sitting still watching and waiting. Usually on a hard floor! Sometimes it's just about being a reassuring presence, creating that space for a mother to do her work. When I attended Batsheva for her fifth birth, she asked me to do nothing but sit quietly in the corner. It reassured her to know I was there, but she likes to labour on her own. As it was too dark to sew, I just sat and pulled wool until she called me to catch the baby. Oh, I was so stiff after that!"

Ruth laughs, "I'm sure you were! Batsheva always was fiercely independent, it's no surprise she births that way." Ruth has a lovely way of seeing a person for their true self. She can read people better than anyone I know and has often helped me better understand an individual's actions by pointing out things about them that I just haven't seen.

"She is," I reply. "She gets it from her mother. I remember my mother telling me Batsheva's mother was just the same. They are a robust line of women!" I add with a chuckle. I'm always very respectful of how a woman wants to labour, I'll be close and hands-on for those who are scared, and keep my distance for those who just want me there in case things take a different path. You can change the course of a birth by not understanding how each mother wants to labour.

"Have the confidence, Salome, to know that some women will not need you," my grandmother would say. "You are there then just to welcome the baby. Always be ready in case your skills are needed, but never feel you have to do something if a woman is labouring well in her own power. This is her journey, not yours."

"Today," I continue lightly, "is about celebration and fun. It's the forty day *mikvah* and a party for Yaffa. We are all going: Martha, Shifra and me."

Today, the fortieth day, we are invited to share in the celebration of the *mikvah,* the ritual cleansing to signal the end of her post-birth seclusion. While we cleanse every month, seven days after our blood-time, the *mikvah* after a birth is a real celebration.

Custom demands that we fully immerse in water. Those near the sea or a river will use them, but as we are up high on a mountain and draw all our water from the well, so it involves a small walk, half a mile or so outside of town, where a natural overhang of rock shelters an entrance to a spring in a low cave. This naturally fills during the wet season but stays full via a slow trickle of water, from a freshwater spring that seeps through the higher mountain, weaving its way through the rocks to this sheltered pool. The hollowed-out area allows you to submerge in it if you sit, then lie down, and the flow of water keeps it fresh enough. There are many of these dotted around the landscape but this one has been designated by the town as the women's cave and it is where we come to *mikvah* both monthly after bleeds but also after the forty days. As a result, we never draw water from this source, for without it we would struggle to fulfil this important ritual.

It is to this spot that Talia and Mary had made the trip about a year before, to mark the end of their confinement. Talia with the many women from her household to support and celebrate with her, and Mary almost alone, having just me and Leah with her. Most days there will be women there. We always go in a group for safety, so it is both spiritually important but also very sociable. On hot days, of which we have so many, it is bliss to crouch under the overhang and enter the cool shade of the cave, feeling the temperature plummet around you. We remove our sandals, outer layers and – protected from external view but under the guarding eyes of the other women – say our prayers and enter the cold water.

Today we have all gathered, female members of Yaffa's family, my-self, Shifra, and Martha, who is soon to be married to Gideon. It is so lovely to bear witness to this ritual marking the end of my care of her, the end of this birthing period, and her return to normal life. There is always a power in women praying together, but especially so when you do it in the light that reflects from the water to the cave roof along with the exhilarating feeling of submersion and renewal.

After Yaffa had completed the *mikvah*, we return to her house for an afternoon of food, prayers, and thanks. Her house is not grand. It's a simple square-shaped building with bare rocks making the walls inside and with a modest courtyard. It is, however, always filled with laughter, children playing and the tools of everyday life. The women and children gather in the courtyard. Tables with brightly coloured cloths quickly fill with food and drinks: fruits, breads, sliced meats and slow-cooked stews. Chatter fills the air, children dart around. Before long the singing begins and so much dancing that my feet start to hurt. The women sing and clap, while a decorated scarf sewn with tiny tinkling pieces of metal is handed round as an invitation to lead the dance. Hips sway making the scarf sing its melody and adding a joyful accompaniment to the dance. Arms and voices are raised in song and laughter. It is such a happy afternoon, babies are passed around, rocked, soothed and jigged by these beautiful, smiling women.

By late afternoon I am ready to head home. Shifra, Martha and I say our goodbyes and step out into the dusty street, laughing, hot, and filled with food and joy. As we round the corner towards the centre of town, we find the streets alive with gossip and excitement. A small desert caravan has arrived and taken up residence on the outskirts of the town. It sits on the flat scrubland opposite the Tower of the Flock. During the afternoon, while we had celebrated in the courtyard of Yaffa's house, a large dark tent, in the style of the nomadic tribes, had been erected on the mountainside, squeezed in around the dotted trees. Fine fabrics of deep red and gold decorate the entrance. A couple of smaller tents for servants and equipment cluster around it. Twenty huge camels, tied to the gnarly trees, rest in the dust.

It does not take long for the whole of Bethlehem to be talking of nothing else. Such excitement! The travellers themselves can occasionally be seen in their fine robes against the sandy landscape. Servants are toing and froing, building fires, cooking or coming into the market to buy fresh provisions. The local children are gathering around the camp, daring each other to go nearer, trying to see who is there and perhaps glimpse something exciting.

We soon learn that this caravan had started from our neighbour in the north, Persia and its last stop had been in Jerusalem as it travelled on the way to Egypt. This was most unexpected, very few caravans stop here. We are too close to Jerusalem to break a journey and not really on the way to anywhere. The excitement their arrival brings is therefore enormous.

Shifra, Martha and I had pieced this much together when we run into Leah on the street. The last year with Joseph, Mary and the baby in the house has softened her features. She has lost that uptight manner that she had held for so many years, and a warmth has come to her that I have never seen before. After greeting us like family, she tells us all she has found out. "Apparently, they are advisors to the Kings of Persia. They are astrologers and holy men. They have asked for an audience with the local rabbis but, I've heard they have come straight from the court of Herod..."

There is always a worry when Herod is involved. While Herod had rebuilt the Temple Mount in Jerusalem and even at one point paid the taxes to the Romans for the Jewish people when we were close to starvation, he had more recently gained a reputation for tyranny and was increasingly held in fear and contempt. His tangled relationship with the Roman leader Mark Anthony, while securing his position, has led many to distrust his loyalty to the Jewish people.

"Any friend of Herod is not a friend of ours," adds Leah dropping her voice in case she is overheard. "What on earth could they want here?" None of us have any idea. Our local rabbis are not the powerful men you find in Jerusalem. There is not enough of a Roman community here for a large temple. The extra soldiers sent during the census have left and those that oversee the town tended to have altars in their homes to the many gods they worship.

Just then, something on the wind catches my attention. A feeling, that strange feeling that there was something, something in the air.

As a midwife I have had these feelings many times, that gut feeling something wasn't right, or a sense that all was going to be well. That unexplained alertness when I was meant to be going to sleep, forecasting (usually accurately) that I would be called out to a birth. It felt as if something was about to happen.

It takes some time to get to our house as we meet so many we know on the way, each with an idea about the strangers pitched at the edge of our town. Yet we are none the wiser as we reach our home and head in to relax after such a lovely day.

I'm in the workshop telling Benjamin about our day when I hear the knock at the door.

As I come out I can make out the shock in Martha's voice as she answers a formal request delivered by a tall robed servant for me to attend the tent to discuss "a matter of importance." By invitation, Benjamin is to accompany me. As we tell him, he is quite excited, he might be a straightforward gentle man but even he cannot not fail to be interested in these visitors.

Leaving the girls with Eitan and Hadar, we wash and prepare. I undo my thick plait and brush out my long dark hair, now showing a scattering of grey. My wide comb made of sticks shaped by Benjamin and woven with thick coloured threads to hold them together, gradually teases the knots from my hair. A tiny bit of fragranced oil smooths the edges and then, winding it round my fingers, over and under, I re-plait it neatly.

I put on my finest dress, a tunic made of dyed dark green cloth with a red stitch around the hem, a lighter green headscarf, and the shawl made for me by Shifra. Benjamin wears a long pale grey tunic and his hemmed cloak. His hair still thick and curly on top, his beard neat and freshly cleaned to remove the sawdust that makes it look lighter than it is. His body, while older, still shows the shape that I have loved for all these years, his shoulders forged by so many years of working wood, are muscular and defined with a spot, my spot, that I cannot help but kiss.

Benjamin shows me three carved wooden goblets. I recognise the wood as oak. Each goblet is patterned with a celestial decoration, a star, the moon, the sun. They are exquisite pieces.

"I thought I would give these to our hosts," he suggests showing me them. "They were for an order, but Joseph and I can make more. It seems fitting for such important visitors. What do you think?"

I nod, it feels right. He had made a goblet with a very similar pattern as a gift for Jesus, that one, though, with a comet on the front. He had said nothing but had listened so quietly and intently when I had told him about this poor couple so far from home, how I suspected Mary had been brought to keep her safe. I told him how brave Mary had been on her own with me in the stable with the animals. On the eighth day, as I was preparing to leave to support her, Benjamin had called me across to the workshop and handed me a gift for the child, a gift made with such thought and love for this little one he had not even met. "May his cup of life always be full," he had said to me as he handed it to me.

The camp is only a few minutes' walk from our house. As we approach, a fragrance of incense wafts over the air, across the dust and the heat of the day. The main tent is as wide as four camels, and I heard it had been erected by just a handful of servants in no time. Dark fabric woven from sheep and camel hair is stretched tight on low diagonal poles, rectangular in shape, with a central high peak dropping around in a gentle slope, reflecting the shape of the mountains behind. Strong ropes secure it to spiral anchors in the ground.

These large tents pack down to a light bundle, the poles bound up and carried by camel to the next site. If there are trees close, they are used to secure ropes. A low entrance takes up a third of the front and is marked by a richly-woven cloth, the red and gold standing out against the dark background. In front waits a man dressed in traditional desert clothing of long tunic, waistcoat and turban. He bows slightly at Benjamin and I as we approach, and ushers us in.

Inside my senses are assailed by scent first and then the colours. The air is thick with the smell of spices, turmeric, frankincense and basil, mixed with the smell of a bundle of sage slowly smoking on a flat rock, the whisps of smoke blue-green as they rise and create shafts wherever the light hits. Overlaying it all is the deep earthy scent of the fabric that envelopes us in the darkness of the tent, such a contrast to the bright light outside. Around the sides of the tent are three huge decorated silk cloths showing constellations of stars and planets. There are inscriptions round the edges in an ornate language I cannot read. I've never seen such cloths outside of the temples in Jerusalem: they are breathtaking, exquisitely patterned and with colours so bold, I cannot imagine what was used to create them. Covering the earth floor are woven reed mats, laid out around a low wooden table made of silky smooth olive wood carried by four upright legs that narrow as they come up through holes on the table top surface, meaning the whole thing can be taken apart and transported. I notice Benjamin eyeing it approvingly.

On the tabletop there are small red pottery bowls filled with dates, pomegranates, grapes and a selection of nuts, offering a note of hospitality. Around the table are a number of cushions to lean on, their dark wool patterns contrasting against the almost sandy ground. It is incredible that all this has been created in an afternoon, carried across the mountains to be packed down and rebuilt at every stop.

From the corner of the tent, three men break off a discussion and come towards us. All are wearing wrapped turbans. Each has a fine cloak worn over a knee length tunic with sandals on their feet. But there the similarity between them ends. The first, a younger African man, his skin not the deep black of those from the land below Egypt but a darker version of our own olive skin. His face oval with tawny brown eyes topped with bushy eyebrows. A small mouth displaying the upturned edges of a frequent smiler, is framed by a trim black beard. His dark red cloak is decorated with large stars woven into the cloth. He bows and introduces himself as Balthazar of the House of Solomon, Ethiopia.

Beside him is an older man, probably the age of myself and Benjamin, but only my height. His hair, silver on olive skin, his face featuring the strong jaw of our Persian neighbours. He introduces himself saying, "I am Melchior, from the court of Phraates the Fourth, priest of Zoroaster, reader of the stars and advisor to the royal families of Persia." He bows slightly, his dark grey tunic folding around him as he does so.

He steps aside to make room for another bearded man in a tunic of a dark blue fabric with a geometric grey weave that with every movement looks like the sea at night. A large nose dominates an otherwise handsome face with dark curly hair and a large beard. His acorn-brown eyes are sharp, but twinkle with a look of fun as he bows and introduces himself, "Gaspar, advisor to the court of Phraates, philosopher, interpreter of dreams and tutor in science and mathematics."

Benjamin and I bow in return and I hear my husband in his quiet deep voice say, "My name is Benjamin, son of Asher, carpenter, and this is my wife Salome, birthkeeper of Bethlehem. Thank you for inviting us. We are deeply honoured."

"Please sit, sit," Balthazar says, gesturing to the cushions. We move to the table and lower ourselves to the ground. Immediately, servants step forward with a bowl and water to wash our hands, holding the bowl underneath as they pour, before another passes a cloth for us to dry them off. We thank the servants and sit nervously, really not sure what might happen next.

"Please eat, drink," Balthazar continues gesturing to the table and we are each passed a goblet, which is quickly filled with a delicious smooth wine that warms the throat and the senses as it slides down.

Being passed the cups reminds Benjamin of his gifts, "Here, these are for you," he says offering the cups to the three men.

The men take them with graciousness and delight at the patterns. "A perfect gift, as we are men of the stars and the skies!" laughs Balthazar gesturing towards the silk sky maps. "What beautiful craftsmanship – you are a skilled man, Benjamin." I feel my reserved husband swell slightly. He would never boast but he is rightly proud of his work.

"Those sky maps are some of the most beautiful things I have ever seen," Benjamin says, partly to deflect the conversation from himself and partly because they are remarkable. "Where are they from? How can such a weave be made? And the colours!"

Gaspar points to the largest one in the middle, a huge great landscape of the sky, dark, almost black shimmery silk with a gold border, numbers and letters surrounding a map of the stars in the sky. Each star is in yellow, gold or silver. Faint lines sewn between them marking shapes, revealing the outline of creatures and figures in the clusters of stars.

"That one is from Chang'an, far to the east, made to my instruction. I was gifted it for services to the Han dynasty. It is my most treasured and useful possession," Gaspar says proudly. "From this, we can understand the movement of the stars above. We can determine what will happen and foresee great events."

"You must be wondering why we have requested your company?" Balthazar says, looking at Benjamin, who nods. But then he turns to me, "It is really your wife we wish to speak to. You are the midwife for the town, are you not?" he asks looking directly at me. I could see that Gaspar and Melchior had stopped and were listening.

"I am, yes, as were my mother and my grandmothers before me," I say with some pride.

"And you attend all the births here?" he asks keenly, as I feel all eyes turn towards me.

"Mostly," I reply, "Very occasionally a family will use a female relative, but my daughters and I have attended every birth in this town these last three years."

He leans forward with an air of excitement, "And you can remember all these babies? Who was born when?"

"I can," I say. "I remember every birth, every mother, every baby born alive or dead." I have absolutely no idea why this might be of interest to these men, but Melchior jumps in.

"There was a star, a joining of the stars over a year ago. We believe that this heralded the arrival of a king, a Jewish king. The star started its journey rising on the horizon low in the sky just before the sun in Aries – this is a sure sign of the birth of a ruler." He pauses for a second, before continuing, "Our role for the Parthian Kings has been to give advice based on what we read in the stars. We believe the prophecy of Micah has been fulfilled –

> *But you, O Bethlehem of Ephrathah, who are one of the*
> *little clans of Judah, from you shall come forth for me*
> *one who is to rule in Israel, whose origin is from of old,*
> *from ancient days...*

I recognise the words from our prophet and am surprised to hear them come from the mouths of these men of other faiths. All three are watching me intently as he asks, "Were there any babies born in this town that night?"

I know precisely who was born that night. There is no need for me to even think about it, but I hesitate for a minute. I know nothing of these men and why they might want the child born that night. I find my courage, "What do you plan to do when you locate the baby?"

The men looked surprised by my question. It is Balthazar who responds first, his response so genuine, his face so transparent, I feel immediately his answer is truthful. "Why we come to honour him, of course!" He pauses, "My family in Ethiopia is from the line of Solomon. A King of the Jews is a King for my people as well."

Melchior sits up straight and adds earnestly, "We come in good faith and with good intent, Mother Salome. My family has served the Court of Kings for generations, advising, teaching and guiding. The signs were so strong for this baby. I wanted to see him myself."

I see Gaspar nodding in agreement, "We have brought gifts and have travelled far to see this child. You have only our word that we mean him no harm, but our word is good." He hesitates and then continues, "We assumed we would be greeting a son of Herod, but we were met there with confusion. Herod asked his advisors and they knew of the prophecy and were interested in the meaning of the joining stars but had not linked the two. Of course…" he laughs amused, a lovely deep chuckle, "they think of our star knowledge as witchcraft, which I assure you it is not – but it meant they had not studied the signs or if they had, were too afraid to tell Herod."

He hesitates again before adding in a most diplomatic tone, "Herod himself seemed very, very interested in this baby and very mistrustful of those around him…" He finishes, "It was most odd that the Jewish leaders of the temple had themselves not come to locate this child."

I look at Benjamin and see the slight nod. The sign that he too believes these men.

I pause, then reply, "The child is Jesus, born to Joseph of Nazareth,

119

a carpenter of the House of David. He and his wife Mary now live with relatives just a short walk from here. Joseph works with my husband, and I count Mary among my friends. But before you go to meet them, may I suggest you speak to Uziel, Chief Shepherd of Migdel Eder. They also were drawn to this child."

At this the three men sit up straight, looking at me then each other with excitement. Gaspar immediately signals to a servant and asks him to send a message to Uziel that they request an audience.

My voice shakes as I say, "This family is not wealthy, not privileged. He is an absolutely lovely child, and they are kind, wonderful parents, but he is a carpenter and she is his wife. They are not royalty. I do not see how this baby can be all you said he is."

I did not mean for so many words to come tumbling out. I feel both disloyal to Jesus and saddened to be so unkind. Then it dawns on me, the words of my mother Levona that somehow, somehow I had forgotten. The words that if I had remembered before I had spoken might have changed what I said. The whole room is looking at me and I feel my shame rising, my face reddening. I add quietly, "Although, as my mother always said," and I look Melchior firmly in the eye, "you never know which baby is another Moses."

It is three days after our meeting with the travellers. Benjamin and I are once again in their company but this time with Leah, Gad, Mary, Joseph and Uziel.

I was not there when the visitors paid their first visit to the house of Leah and Gad, to see Gad nearly burst with pride. He made sure all the neighbours saw these important guests at his door, as they arrived with an entourage of servants. Behind them, a hoard of excited children, cramming to see the colourful visitors. Three days later and Benjamin and I have been invited to help with the discussion.

Today we are all once again in the large tent, we have not long arrived and been made welcome. The travelling men, Joseph, Uziel, Benjamin, Leah, Mary and I, crowd round the low table. The young infant Jesus has been left with Shifra, who will entertain him while we talk. The food and drink are once again generous, but this time the discussion is heated. Leah is sitting next to me, Mary on my other side as the debate about Jesus continues.

Leah leans in towards me and fills me in, her voice almost a whisper, "They arrived with gifts the day after they met you. Gold, frankincense and myrrh for the little one. Stunning gifts, precious gifts, but really, they asked questions – many, many questions. Who was the grandfather and the great-grandfather of Joseph? Of Mary? How far back could the family be traced?"

She continues, "They seem to be trying to work out the importance of this child. Days of discussion and questions. It has been very heated."

Mary is close enough to hear and adds, her voice urgent, "They came, I think, expecting a king. When we were, well, as we are, they wanted to know everything about both of our families. And now they want to take my child!"

I gasp, perhaps too loud as it turns the attention of the room towards us.

The men break off from introductory chatter. It is Gaspar who leads. "Thank you for coming, Benjamin, Salome," he nods towards as us. "We are here," he continues, "to discuss the child, Jesus. This child that the stars told us would be born here, and indeed we found here, under the joined stars. He fulfils the prophesy of Micah."

Melchior jumps in, "We believe this child is destined for greatness, and great leaders need shaping. He must be trained as a prince would be. So, you understand, Salome and Benjamin, while Joseph and Mary have been wonderful parents to this point, they cannot prepare the boy for the life ahead of him. We, though, as advisors to kings, can."

Balthazar then adds his part, his voice kindly, "This is why we have come: to offer our services to this prophesied king. We have trained and prepared princes in some of the most important families. This is what men like us do: we make kings. We believe that we should take the boy and raise him in preparation for his destined life. We would value your thoughts, as we are struggling to persuade Joseph and Mary of this."

Joseph, gentle calm Joseph, however is shaking his head. "This is our son. He needs to be with us. You cannot take him away from his parents! He needs to be brought up with us, with his people in his community, as a Jewish boy, taught our ways and taught a craft."

Gaspar sounds exasperated as he replies, "But think of what we can offer him! Learning, science, philosophy… We can introduce him to important people."

I notice Joseph is muttering, "No, no," as he shakes his head.

It is Mary who then speaks up for her son, "But what will he become? God gave us this child. He knew who we were. Will he stay faithful to his Jewish upbringing if he is removed from it? Whose values will he be brought up with? He will be taught like a prince, but have no power, no land, no protection."

This causes a stir in the room and a flurry of talk. Leah is nodding and reaches over to hold Mary's hand.

"We were drawn to this child," Uziel interjects, "but he was born to these parents, to their care. If the Almighty has chosen them, who are we to overrule that?"

"May I speak?" asks Benjamin. "There has to be a reason we are all here for this child. Perhaps this life here is God's plan." He says quietly, "It's like carpentry. The wood has to be allowed to grow, it needs good soil, water, sun, enough wind to test the strength, to harden it up but not to snap it. Then when it reaches the right age, you and I take that wood Joseph, and we shape it, smooth it, turn it into something of purpose and use. It remains the wood it was, but now it is in service. It has to grow strong first. You cannot tell from a sapling how big a tree will grow."

Joseph nods in agreement – I see Gaspar and Balthazar exchange a whisper.

"Perhaps," I say hesitantly, "perhaps, there is another way. Let the boy be a child, learn his father's skill. See how he grows. Let us see if there are signs the prophecy is true." I look at the three travellers. "Write to him if you want, do not be strangers. When he is older, if it is fitting, he can come to you then."

My words have silenced the room. You can almost hear them being weighed, considered. Melchior, Balthazar and Gaspar exchange looks and tentative nods. I see Leah's shoulders drop, Uziel is nodding very slightly as he considers the idea. The murmurs in the room are now sounding more positive.

The atmosphere slowly changes from one of conflict to one of agreement. Gradually we work it out, these advisors to kings, the carpenters, leathermaker, midwife and women. The child will remain with Mary and Joseph. All three of the Magi offer their services to the boy, to write to him as he grows older, sharing their wisdom and counsel. Melchior who gave the gift of gold, offering his knowledge of philosophy; Gaspar who had given the gift of frankincense, lessons in the celestial world, mathematics and science; and finally, Balthazar, who had gifted the child myrrh, that precious resin so associated with the leaving of this world, from him the offer of theology.

After the three men had offered their services, Uziel spoke again, "I shall be here to counsel the boy. I shall teach him the way of the Shepherds of the Flock. Just as these holy teachings were shared with me. When he is old enough, I can also ensure an introduction to the temple priests in Jerusalem."

As they prepare to leave, each of the Magi leaves the child with a scroll marked with their seal that gives the boy a promise of support and guidance. They offer their service to this child born under a star, their letter and seal allowing him passage to them if he should ever need it.

Balthazar turns to Mary and Joseph as he hands his over, "When he is old enough, give him these. They reflect the promise we make him today. Our wisdom is his wisdom, our duty is in his service. May God protect this child and his family and may the plan that God has for him be fulfilled."

The king-makers have given their gifts.

I cannot imagine what the plan is for this beautiful, bouncy little one. He is right now off with Shifra totally oblivious to the decisions being made about his life. He's still just a baby and yet so much importance is being placed on him. It's still all so surprising that this ordinary family should be the cause of such discussions.

I pray for the boy, that he will have goodness and good judgement in abundance for the life ahead of him. What if he *is* another Moses? Moses himself was born to an ordinary family. God can make anything ordinary become extraordinary if it is His will. Moses was saved from death when *he* was put into the reed basket. All those Hebrew babies died and yet *he* was the one to survive. It was he who went on to bring our people to the Promised Land.

A sudden shiver crosses me. The thought of the mother of Moses setting her child out on the river in a desperate attempt to save him always upsets me, but it's not that making me shiver. A feeling. A fear. I do not know what of. But God put a princess of Egypt there to find Moses, perhaps he also put these wise men here for Jesus. I pray under my breath to protect the child.

With His wing He will cover you, and under His wings
you will take refuge; His truth is an encompassing shield.
You will not fear the fright of night, the arrow that flies
by day.

Stars, seals, king-makers.

I put my arm around Mary and give her a comforting squeeze. All these things for her child, her beloved baby boy. It's overwhelming when you think too much on it. How can this all be?

When life is the same day-to-day we sometimes wish for more excitement, for something amazing to happen. Right now, it's hard not to pray for the opposite. For a simple life for this boy. No travelling Magi. No prophetic stars, just an everyday life.

Mary reaches out for my other hand on my lap and gently squeezes it back. She looks me in the eye, "Thank you, Salome. We must trust in God. He has certainly already gifted us with so many to help and guide his journey."

It is true. I look around at us all gathered in this remarkable tent. All there for this baby born under a star.

Epilogue

As we wash the battered, lifeless body of Jesus, his face is so swollen he looks like a grotesque version of himself. One eye nearly closed with swelling, blood stains round his head where those monsters had rammed thorns into his flesh. There are cuts across his back from the whip, and of course the great gaping holes where nails had been driven through his hands and feet. How can this be the body of that baby we washed and swaddled together all those years ago, on that quiet, still night? His body then so tiny, his skin still wet from the waters of birth, to this tortured man's body in front of us. I do not know where Mary found the strength to see her beloved son in such a state. I was so glad Joseph was no longer alive to face this utter heart-break.

As always now, when washing the dead, I remember Martha, Shifra and I washing the body of my beloved Benjamin when he had died. His old skin so different from the firm olive skin of Jesus. Benjamin's was weathered from the years, wrinkled and marked. With Benjamin we washed his skin and rubbed oils across the arms that had worked for us, held us, hugged us, and touched us. It was both heart-breaking and healing. To care for his body but with each touch of his lifeless form realising that he really had gone. Saying goodbye with loving touch to every part of the man who had been my companion, friend and lover for over forty years. That day I could let Benjamin go. We'd had so many good years and he had looked so peaceful, the lines on his face softened in death. While my heart was lost and broken as I faced life without my husband and soulmate, I knew it was his time to go and could be thankful for so many beautiful years together.

Today though, wrapping Jesus was nothing like that. The searing, visceral pain of seeing his life ripped from him, his body so abused, this beloved child dead before us, was almost too much to bear.

I had stood with Mary when he had died. Our lives had remained intertwined over the thirty or so years since the night they fled. The day we lost all those boys. How can you forget that? How could my heart not go with this mother who knew forever, every single time that she looked at her son, that so many mothers would never get to look at their boys again. The infants so brutally murdered in the hunt for her child. Her son had lived. But thirty-two infant boys in our town had died that awful day. Nightmares of the screams still wake me on occasion, even thirty years on. The agonising scream from the infants as the blade ran through them, the terror and grief of the mothers, shock and horror making them sound like wild animals. I have never before or since heard such pain: fathers, brothers, sisters, aunts, uncles emitting gut wrenching howls of agony. Even now, after all these years, every so often the smell of blood, or the glimmer of a sword on a belt will transport me, horror-struck, back to that scene from hell itself.

That day a light was stamped out in our town and it took so many years to rekindle. Tiny Arran, Denah's infant boy, lived only those few precious months before he was dragged from her arms and slaughtered. I supported Denah through the next three births, all quick, all girls. Her stoicism got her through, but her joy never returned in full. Talia went on to have two more sons and three daughters, but the weight she carried from the horror dimmed her light, as though a piece of her heart was always in pain, still screaming, as she did when she held the lifeless, bloodied body of her young boy.

That fateful event came just the day after the discussions with the three Magi about the future of Jesus. Joseph had come to see Benjamin and me later that evening. He had been working with Benjamin and Eitan for over a year. Having proved himself a skilled craftsman, they found that with three of them they could take on bigger tasks and earn enough to support us all. I'd seen him master his craft under the tutelage of my Benjamin, so kind and generous my husband was with his knowledge. With Mary's visits making her feel part of the family, Jesus had become like a grandchild to me.

It was dark when Joseph had appeared ashen-faced at the door and told of a terrifying dream in which Jesus was in mortal danger. He had assumed it was just that, a bad dream, until Balthazar had returned to their house and warned them that all three of the Magi had the same vision. They had consulted the charts and feared the dreams were true: Herod planned to harm the child and they must flee with Jesus immediately. The Magi had agreed they would not return as they had promised to Herod's palace, but would instead travel to Persia via a different route and offered Mary and Joseph passage in their caravan heading south.

A panicked Mary and Joseph had packed their belongings and, leaving a distraught Leah who had come alive this last year with them in the house, were ready to go. They were just waiting for the cover of darkness to make their escape.

Joseph had come to say goodbye and collect his tools. He'd left Mary and Jesus hiding in a nearby cave on the outskirts of town, slightly away from buildings in case someone came looking for them. They were to meet the Magi just outside of Bethlehem that night, with a plan to head south into Egypt where members of Gaspar's family would keep them safe. I remember our confusion and upset. How Benjamin had wept as he said goodbye, helping Joseph pack his tools, and pressing a bag of coins into his hands. I wrapped my shawl around me and put my scarf on, insisting that I accompanied him at least to the cave to say goodbye. I felt safe going with him, as in my role I frequently moved around the town at night. No questions would be asked or anything unusual noticed.

This is how I got to say goodbye to Mary. She was huddled in the corner of the cave, their meagre belongings in rolls at her feet. She was trying to keep Jesus quiet by feeding him. Of course, as soon as Jesus heard my voice, he came off the breast and turned to smile at me, letting a small shower of milk spray the sandy rocks around. It took much to keep him quiet as I kissed his head all over and held Mary so tight, weeping my goodbye. I felt my heart would break as they crept off into the night.

I thought that was the worst. But it was nothing. Nothing compared to the morning when the soldiers came and butchered the infant boys of our town. I cannot imagine how Mary must have felt when she heard what had happened. The pain of it, the knowledge that it was her son they came for. What a burden to carry.

When they left, I did not see her for another ten years. After Herod died, they left Egypt to return and settle in Nazareth. Mary sent a message through a cousin of Gad, who was returning to Bethlehem that they would be attending the temple in Jerusalem for *Shavuot*, so I made plans to visit family and meet them there. Oh, the joy to see them safe and well and hold them in my arms!

To my surprise, Mary knew the name of each child who had been killed. She knew the name of each mother and asked me about every family with a sadness and love I cannot convey. She asked me about them every time we met, even though our meetings would be years apart. She never forgot a single name.

I was very old when Jesus was arrested, Benjamin had been dead five long years by then. I found out only by chance, from a neighbour recently returned from Jerusalem. The following Jesus had was widely talked about. Many from our village had been to hear him preach. I had too, as often as I could. He was tall like his father but had a presence far beyond that of either of his parents. I had watched the crowd tuning into his words with a respectful quiet, whereas normally a large crowd listening to a preacher will chatter, eat and wander around, his followers did not. They calmed and listened to his stories told in his deep voice, his accent altered by the places he had lived. A trace of Egyptian, a Galilean lilt, a Bethlehem vowel. His lessons so beautiful: acceptance, kindness, forgiveness, love. With the brutality of the Romans that we have lived under for so many years, his message was balm to the soul, a different way to live, a kinder way to be.

His mother was usually with him when he preached, and she and I would always catch up. Shifra, Martha and Hadar had all come along to hear him at varying points with their families. We were always made welcome by the group he travelled with, his closest companions John and Miriam of Magdela, a fine-looking Jewish woman of good background, were always delightful company.

By the end, the crowds that followed him were huge. The Romans had started to take notice but not as much as the those who worked to keep their control in Jerusalem. I knew in my heart immediately that his arrest was dangerous, that those who conspired against him would not miss an opportunity to rid themselves of him.

In my younger days, the journey to Jerusalem would have been walkable, but my bones are old and my walking unsteady, so I borrowed a donkey from a neighbour and got my grandson Gavriel, a fine young man with a look of his grandfather Benjamin, to accompany me and deliver me to the house of our cousin.

Mary was easy to find, the town talked of nothing else but the imprisonment of Jesus, and the women that followed him were known by others we knew. Once I got a message to her, I was brought to her and ushered through with haste by one of her son's followers. Her beautiful dark hair was now silver and her skin wrinkled, but that smile and her eyes were the same, even with the worry etched across her face.

I do not wish to remember watching them kill that poor boy. The horror of it will stay with me forever, as I stood with Mary, Miriam of Magdala and their friends, all holding each other up, trying not to scream and praying for a miracle that somehow this nightmare would stop, that he would be saved.

But it didn't. And he wasn't.

We watched as he slumped in death and his side was pierced. I felt Mary's knees go and heard the bone chilling sob of Miriam as it ended, the sky darkening as though it reflected the grief we felt.

I'm not sure how long it was before we got his body. When we thought we would not be allowed it, hope came in the name of a man called Joseph of Arimathea, a follower of Jesus. He was an unimposing man, small in stature, but polite, well-mannered and respectful. Somehow, in all the upset, chaos, and suspicion, he got permission to have Jesus' body released and offered a tomb to put it in.

Time was short, Jesus had to be wrapped and buried before the sunset on Passover Eve.

Mary, Miriam and I together had the task of preparing the body, as is the custom. Miriam, her beautiful face contorted with pain and grief, had a jar of precious oil and myrrh. She had held it with her at Golgotha, clutching the bag close to her as if it was a protection against the horror unfolding in front of us. She had stayed when other disciples of Jesus had fled. She had stood with his mother and watched it all. I felt her body shaking with fear and recoil in pain every time Jesus stumbled or was beaten. Now she clutched the bag still, knuckles white as she tried to gather herself for the task ahead. Another Mary, the mother of James, who had also been at the crucifixion, came to the mouth of the tomb with aromatic herbs: olive, laurel, palm and cypress for us lay on the body.

I have no idea who brought the wrapping, but his broken body was laid on that cold slab in the tomb before us and we had this one chance to get him ready and say goodbye. When he was a baby, his body was so tiny it had not taken his mother and I long to oil and swaddle him. Now, even with three pairs of hands, it took time, trying to see through tears, to hold back the huge waves of horror and bring ourselves to lay hands on him.

So strong was the grief and distress that I couldn't tell you who started the song. It was a lament that would break your heart on the lightest of days, but at that moment its expression of grief helped us. The beautiful sound of this song of sorrow echoing around the tomb gave us the strength to touch, to wash, to oil and to wrap his broken body, laying on the herbs and swaddling him just as his mother and I had when he was baby. Mary and Miriam were the last to kiss his battered head before it too was wrapped, gently laying him back on the rock, touching his heart and whispering prayers and goodbyes.

We left, still deeply in song, a wailing, heart-breaking outpouring, stepping out into the setting sun, just we women. There at his birth and now his death, thinking that was the end...

The journey of a midwife in a family's life may only last a few hours, but it can last a lifetime. For most of the thousands of babies I have helped into the world, I have been with their mother through the pregnancy, through the birth and at least the forty days afterwards. I have been privy and witness to so much.

From secrets to surprises, loss, healing, heartache and so much joy. I have stood in awe, time and time again, as women walk the hot coals of birth, finding from deep within the power to open up and bring forth life. It remains to me the most sacred moment: life and death, before and after, unknown to known, hidden to seen. It should be the most sacred event for a woman, we are blessed with a moment of creation from God Himself. This should be treated with the highest respect and care. Each child welcomed with reverence.

"You never know which baby is another Moses," my mother would say in her beautiful low voice. "Who are you to know which baby will change everything and maybe save a people, perhaps save our people again? All babies must be welcomed as if they were the One."

The night when Moses was born his mother cannot have imagined what a future he would have, what a difference he would make to our people.

How also could we have known that still, calm night in Bethlehem how special that baby would prove to be?

I remember every one of the births and all the babies I served in my life. I hope, as I walk my path towards closing my eyes one last time and joining my beautiful Benjamin, that I honoured those words throughout my life, treating every baby as the One. For every baby, but especially, that night when the stars joined over Bethlehem. When something as simple as the birth of a baby brought such pain and yet... So much change, so much love; such a remarkable time. Such a baby.

THE END

Afterword

Across time women's stories have been forgotten, and so it is with this – one of the most famous births. I wanted to give voice to one special woman, in memory of all those midwives and birthkeepers who came before and after. While the details are imagined, it is a story informed by practices across the world and over time. Through Salome's eyes we see the true power of midwifery and the transformational journey of birth.

Pregnancy is a special time. In so many cultures throughout history it has been regarded as a sacred time with practices of protection around pregnant women and during birth. We've lost much of this respect for the journey of pregnancy and birth as rite of passage, a transformational moment. That is a huge loss.

What happens during birth matters, it's when mothers and fathers are forged, birthed in the fire of labour. They can be empowered and enabled or left traumatised by the experience, all by how they are treated. The journey matters, not just the outcome. Birth is a rite of passage, it can empower and enrich lives. It's a sacred time and we treat it like a medical procedure.

This needs to change.

Obstructed childbirth

In Yaffa's birth she is in danger of an obstructed birth.

Prolonged and obstructed childbirth can cause an obstetric fistula. Each year between 50,000 to 100,000 women worldwide are affected by obstetric fistula, an abnormal opening between a woman's genital tract and her urinary tract or rectum. It leaves survivors leaking urine or faeces – and sometimes both – through their vagina.

Women who experience obstetric fistula suffer constant incontinence. Sufferers of obstetric fistula are often subject to severe social stigma due to their smell and perceptions of uncleanliness. In many cases women are then divorced by their husbands, abandoned by their families and even outcast by their communities. It is estimated that more than 2 million young women live with untreated obstetric fistula in Asia and sub-Saharan Africa.

For a population of over 112 million, Ethiopia has fewer than 626 obstetricians/gynaecologists, and whilst huge progress has been made in recent years, there are still fewer than 17,000 trained midwives working in Ethiopia. Fewer than 30% of Ethiopian women receive any form of care from a skilled childbirth attendant. A USAID study found that an estimated 36,000 to 39,000 women in Ethiopia live with obstetric fistula, and over 3,000 additional new cases occur each year. With surgery these women can be helped and restored to health.

If this book has moved you to donate, please go to:
ethiopiaid.org.uk or hamlinfistulauk.org
to treat a woman in Ethiopia with a fistula today.

Acknowledgements

I would like to thank my mother, Christine Supple, for a lifetime of love and inspiration as a wonderful role model and for the positive messages about birth, as well as the beautiful postnatal care she gave us when our babies were new. To my wonderful father, Edmund Supple, for a love of learning, stories and adventure. Thank you for your patience editing and help with my apparently appalling punctuation!

Special thanks to my lovely sister Emma and sister-in-law Emily for both walking through the fires of birth with me and for all the love and support over the years. To my brother Tom, for being a wonderful human and brilliant brother.

A huge thank you to Lucy Pearce of Womancraft Publishing for breaking all her rules and giving my story a chance. I love how you've helped me craft this book.

For help with editing my first draft and for her never-ending supply of enthusiasm, Felicity Wingrove of Zen Communications who embraces creativity with an infectious positivity. To Alan Adams for so generously sharing your knowledge.

My cousin, Ruth Supple, for her fantastic input, who helped me see my words for what they could be. At the very start of this process I was helped enormously by Antonia Prescott who took time to help me formulate my style and round the story. To Joanna Summers who worked a magic she might not have realised when she told me I had to write this book.

To the amazing team of antenatal teachers I not only trained with but have had the privilege of working with serving the families of Birmingham for seventeen years. Special thanks to Amy Maclean, Helen Knight, Lynn Frost, Joanna Summers, Delia Stokes, Isabelle Karimov and Rachel Nolan. Thank you all for sharing your wisdom and so much laughter. Special mention to Sue Woollett for sharing antenatal knowledge and supporting all my initiatives! To Sophie Messager for adding to my Closing the Bones knowledge, providing a wealth of postnatal practice wisdom and incredibly useful insights as the book developed.

To Professor Mary Nolan (Professor of Perinatal Education at the University of Worcester) for being not only my own NCT antenatal teacher, but then tutor and now my colleague at the International Journal of Birth and Parent Education (www.ijbpe.com) and friend. Your influence on my journey has been enormous. To Shona Gore who I first met nearly twenty years ago at my NCT induction and for the last eight years with the IJBPE, thank you for the wealth knowledge you generously share and unflagging support and interest.

To Rabbi Debbi Young-Somers, thank you for taking the time to read my work and help me be clear on Jewish practices, and to Francesca Rose, Linda De Lange and Deborah Sibley, NCT antenatal teachers who gave so generously of their time, thoughts and insights as Jewish women.

To Father Bill Jenkinson (priest and family friend in Malawi) and Father Shaw of St Helen's Crosby who practiced and taught me a Catholicism based on joy, inclusion and love.

To all the wonderful NCT colleagues who have shared knowledge and skills over the years. To retired Consultant Midwife Paula Clark for her incredible, inspirational focus on woman-centred care. Supporting me through my own VBAC births and founding the BWH Birth Centre and Homebirth team. Birmingham families lost out when you retired.

To Selina Wallis for the doula retreats and sharing your knowledge about the biomechanics of birth. To one of my oldest and dearest friends Nicola Garrett, for supporting me during my youngest's birth, but also for pressing a copy of *The Continuum Concept* into my hands as a new mother. Thanks to Damien Cunningham for listening to my theories about the Magi and helping me formulate my thoughts. More thanks for endless patience as I brought every conversation back to the book to Kirsten Faith, Caron Malcom and Tracey Clark-Hill!

Thanks to Brigitta Shuker of Studio Yi Shrewsbury who generously gave me traditionally dyed wool to make an authentic dyed red thread bracelet.

I've been so lucky to train with some of the most influential traditional childbirth figures and have to add my thanks to Robin Lim (Bumi Sehat) for birth wisdom, Angelina Martinez Miranda (traditional midwifery), and Dr Rocio Alarcon from Ecuador (rebozo and Closing the Bones), all who helped me learn techniques, skills, customs and a respect for the wisdom handed down for generations. I've also learnt from some of the greats of childbirth such as Ina May Gaskin, Mary Cronk (breech workshop), Sheila Kitzinger (birth trauma workshop), Jean Sutton (optimal fetal positioning workshop), Andrea Robinson (childbirth education), The Indie Birth team, Gail Tully (Spinning Babies) and Ingula Rinkevičienė for organizing a fantastic birth wisdom event in Lithuania and practicing as an authentic birthkeeper.

To all the parents who have shared their pregnancy and parenting journey with me and those who asked me to accompany them during their birth. I've learnt so much as well as, I hope, been a help attending births as a doula support.

To my dearest friends Liz Bushell, Tracy Waldron-Pegge and Marie

Monk-Hawksworth for love, friendship, adventures and support, I really am so blessed have you in my life.

Finally, my huge thanks to my husband David, who has supported me and my drive to support women and families through the birth and parenting journey for the last twenty years. Thank you honey, love you. To Lisa-Marie Müller, my amazing host daughter who has been a sounding board for so many wonderful projects and enriched our lives. Lastly my children, Alexander, Estella, Cassie and Zachary, who have been and remain my inspiration and joy.

About the Author

Like Salome, Bridget Supple has devoted her life to supporting women through all stages of pregnancy, labour, and parenting. A mother of four herself, she works as an antenatal teacher for the NCT, the NHS, in particular for Birmingham Women's Hospital and Birth Companions, a charity supporting pregnant women in prison. She is the founder of an information resource all about the Infant Microbiome (babysbiome.org) and runs workshops on parenting, brain development and hypnobirthing. She has also worked on the International Journal of Birth and Parent Education (ijbpe.com) for over eight years. Bridget lives in Shropshire with her husband and four children.

About Womancraft

Womancraft Publishing was founded on the revolutionary vision that women and words can change the world. We act as midwife to transformational women's words that have the power to challenge, inspire, heal and speak to the silenced aspects of ourselves.

We believe that:

○ books are a fabulous way of transmitting powerful transformation,

○ values should be juicy actions, lived out,

○ ethical business is a key way to contribute to conscious change.

At the heart of our Womancraft philosophy is fairness and integrity. Creatives and women have always been underpaid. Not on our watch! We split royalties 50:50 with our authors. We work on a full circle model of giving and receiving: reaching backwards, supporting Tree-Sisters' reforestation projects, and forwards via Worldreader, providing books at no cost to education projects for girls and women.

We are proud that Womancraft is walking its talk and engaging so many women each year via our books and online. Join the revolution! Sign up to the mailing list at womancraftpublishing.com and find us on social media for exclusive offers:

(f) womancraftpublishing

womancraft_publishing

womancraftpublishing.com/books

Use of Womancraft Work

Often women contact us asking if and how they may use our work. We love seeing our work out in the world. We love you sharing our words further. And we ask that you respect our hard work by acknowledging the source of the words.

We are delighted for short quotes from our books – up to 200 words – to be shared as memes or in your own articles or books, provided they are clearly accompanied by the author's name and the book's title.

We are also very happy for the materials in our books to be shared amongst women's communities: to be studied by book groups, discussed in classes, read from in ceremony, quoted on social media... with the following provisos:

o If content from the book is shared in written or spoken form, the book's author and title must be referenced clearly.

o The only person fully qualified to teach the material from any of our titles is the author of the book itself. There are no accredited teachers of this work. Please do not make claims of this sort.

o If you are creating a course devoted to the content of one of our books, its title and author must be clearly acknowledged on all promotional material (posters, websites, social media posts).

o The book's cover may be used in promotional materials or social media posts. The cover art is copyright of the artist and has been licensed exclusively for this book. Any element of the book's cover or font may not be used in branding your own marketing materials when teaching the content of the book, or content very similar to the original book.

o No more than two double page spreads, or four single pages of any book may be photocopied as teaching materials.

We are delighted to offer a 20% discount of over five copies going to one address. You can order these on our webshop, or email us. If you require further clarification, email us at: info@womancraftpublishing.com

Sisters of the Solstice Moon

Gina Martin

Book 1 of the When She Wakes series

On the Winter Solstice, thirteen women across the world see the same terrifying vision. Their world is about to experience ravaging destruction. All that is now sacred will be destroyed. Each answers the call, to journey to Egypt, and save the wisdom of the Goddess. This is the history before history. This is herstory, as it emerged.

An imagining… or is it a remembering… of the end of matriarchy and the emergence of global patriarchy, this book brings alive long dead cultures from around the world and brings us closer to the lost wisdoms that we know in our bones.

Muddy Mysticism: The Sacred Tethers of Body, Earth and Everyday

Natalie Bryant Rizzieri

Muddy Mysticism is a spiritual memoir, a lyrical articulation of an emergent feminist mysticism and a heartfelt response to the lack of mystical literature by women who have chosen a life of family, love, work and the world. Like many women she found the faith of her childhood no longer fitted… yet still there is a longing for the sacred. Through poetry, reflection and experience she moves into the possibility of direct experience with the divine… beyond a belief system. Exploring the possibility of daily life in the modern world not as something to be transcended or escaped… but as a mystical path in its own right.

Made in United States
North Haven, CT
26 November 2024

60930976R00093